PENGUIN BOOKS

Volume 1

Volume 1

New Voices from a Diverse Culture

Foreword by David Lammy, MP

PENGUIN BOOKS

PENGUIN BOOKS

Published by the Penguin Group
Penguin Books Ltd, 80 Strand, London WC2R 0RL, England
Penguin Group (USA) Inc., 375 Hudson Street, New York, New York 10014, USA
Penguin Group (Canada), 90 Eglinton Avenue East, Suite 700, Toronto, Ontario, Canada M4P 2Y3
(a division of Pearson Penguin Canada Inc.)
Penguin Ireland, 25 St Stephen's Green, Dublin 2, Ireland
(a division of Penguin Books Ltd)
Penguin Group (Australia), 250 Camberwell Road, Camberwell, Victoria 3124, Australia
(a division of Pearson Australia Group Pty Ltd)
Penguin Books India Pvt Ltd, 11 Community Centre, Panchsheel Park, New Delhi – 110 017, India
Penguin Group (NZ), 67 Apollo Drive, Mairangi Bay, Auckland 1310, New Zealand
(a division of Pearson New Zealand Ltd)
Penguin Books (South Africa) (Pty) Ltd, 24 Sturdee Avenue, Rosebank, Johannesburg 2196, South Africa

Penguin Books Ltd, Registered Offices: 80 Strand, London WC2R 0RL, England

www.penguin.com

First published in Penguin Books 2006
2

Selection copyright © Penguin Books, 2006
Copyright for each piece lies with individual authors © 2006
Foreword copyright © David Lammy, 2006
All rights reserved

The moral right of the authors has been asserted

With acknowledgements to decibel and Arts Council England

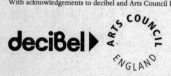

Set in 11/13 pt Monotype Dante
Typeset by Rowland Phototypesetting Ltd, Bury St Edmunds, Suffolk
Printed in England by Clays Ltd, St Ives plc

ISBN-13: 978-0-141-02702-9

Contents

Foreword

I am delighted to have been asked to provide the foreword for this collection of brilliant short stories by unpublished British writers of African, Asian and Caribbean descent.

We are known all over the world as a country that produces great writers. Our best contemporary authors undoubtedly draw on a vast back-catalogue of English literature, but are also influenced by many other cultures, traditions and countries. In this environment we are familiar with the novels of bestselling authors such as Zadie Smith and Monica Ali, but these are only the tip of an iceberg that consists of a wide range of writers who have emerged from the migrant communities in recent years.

A staggering number and variety of writers from this background are now a central part of the canon of contemporary English literature – Nadeem Aslam and Diran Adebayo, Tahir Shah and Meera Syal, Kunal Basu and Malorie Blackman, Andrea Levy and Mike Phillips, and there are many more – each one writing from a distinct and individual perspective. At the same time, these writers offer us a new and unique insight into what it means to be British, while creating, within the content of English literature, new subject matters, new approaches to the language, and new ways of seeing the world which we all inhabit.

This collection of short stories does the same. Set against a variety of backgrounds, each story gives a valuable glimpse into someone else's world, from the comical thoughts of a teenage boy to moving tales of displacement. What is absolutely clear from these stories is that ethnic and cultural diversity continues to enrich British fiction. As the MP for Tottenham, the most diverse constituency anywhere in Europe, I see at first hand the breadth of experience and cultures that makes up the richness of our national identity. Reflecting that diversity in British fiction can only be a good thing. It is something I wholeheartedly support. The decibel Penguin Anthology is so important because it celebrates this diversity, and also gives previously unpublished writers a platform. In doing this it brings to the attention of readers work that might not otherwise cross their radars. I believe all this adds up to a more generous, more eclectic, more interesting cultural palette.

I am endlessly inspired by the quality of the modern writing that I see. But I also know that getting published is incredibly difficult. Publishers, booksellers, librarians and Arts Council England all have a responsibility to nurture and promote the works of new and exciting writers. I hope that through this anthology, and other similar initiatives, the process will become a little easier for some.

For all these reasons, I am delighted to introduce this decibel Penguin Anthology. I hope that the work of these new writers will soon appear on many bookshelves and that you will find these short stories as captivating and thought-provoking as I have.

David Lammy

DAVID LAMMY, MP

Flyover Stalker

Sylvia Jean Dickinson

Outside the Waterfront fences, the motorway runs into an unfinished flyover. A leaping hyena sprawled in mid-air, caught between seafront and the Foreshore high-rises. Circling traffic hums, blind to this bridge. Its cement pylons hold arches hiding riff-raff rows of homes tacked from bummed boards for a hodgepodge of people, leathered by sun and by birth. Hansie lies on his litter of rags in his one-man shack. Listens to sundown guffaw. As night blackens, noises quicken, roughen to brawl. Rubs a black pebble, says in his head, 'Doss down,' shuts out the bawling. Twists to sleep, dreaming slow night hours in strange places. Shivers awake, clammy in summer's misty dawning, rises long-long before bridge-people stir.

Their day starts at ten, sometimes eleven. They're unofficial attendants who patrol parking bays. Cash upfront, the car slips into the slot. Sometimes, old tourists stray into the bridge tracks, dig into pockets, flip a rand or two into cupped hands. Toothless grins may nod, 'Dankie, my baas.' Fall about cackling after foreigners, who escape, clutching cameras, feeling for wallets.

Bridge-people say, 'Hey, Hansie, is you getting up more gek than you was? Hell, man, goin to work!' They chuckle as he lowers his head, beams with them, not understanding their jokes.

For he's a young man. Proud of his job. Who cracks out at eight, collecting his cart at the City Corporation yard. A street-sweeper; shaking his head at dust brought by rattling skiddonks or sleek limousines. What hooks him is a snorting sports-mobile. The blonde chick driver, with sparklers for ears, stops. Zapps up her radio, reggae hammers the street. Hansie brushes his broom in time to the beat bucking, blurts, 'Crazee.' It doddles his day. He finishes at five, cavorts home, the fast car flashing red in his head.

Under the arches, night thumps with beats on boxes, piercing penny whistles and harmonized voices, drumming Africa into bridge-people's feet. Round two in the morning, when the galley embers ashen, the sweet dagga scent dies, the empties scatter, Hansie nimbles the gap in the rolled barbed-wire girder blocking the start of the flyover's slope. Takes off his shirt, gasps the sea breeze. It sticks to his skin. Gazes as the Devil stokes his pipe, smoke furling mountains lining the city bowl.

From his flyover, Hansie scans Signal Hill, Lion's Head, Table Mountain, Devil's Peak and freeway. Rubs a black pebble. Fancies his perch is a red coupé. Mounts, brakes where the road suddenly stops.

Dismounts, cries, 'Run!' Swells, splits through his skin, springs into silk sunrise. Zings over the pass. Recalls veld camp-fire stories that mix in the mist. Sees Knysna's forests of elephants, Big Bull's tusks crushing thickets. Hansie jumps swamps that can suck in a man. And he's a lone troubadour, possessing the land. Caresses her hills, wallows through valleys. Zigzags back over treacherous tracks. Reaches the bridge, idles, cooling on the flyover's hump. By five, Hansie's down in his shack, dreaming to the bridge-people's snoring. No one notices Hansie's been gone.

Others from the city are afraid to enter the shadows under the bridge. Local social workers think they might be attacked. Police drive up in packs, only when forced by townspeople's complaints about noise, theft or filth.

One Monday, when the camp's still dizzy with sleep, a visitor comes: Miss Molly Dogood on some student exchange with cash from the British Council. 'A major priority,' she says, 'is Portakabin latrines.' Where she's from, dog shit's OK, but human excrement's the pits. 'And,' she says, 'you can make yourself better.' Hansie rubs his stubble, says, 'Please, Merrem Dogood, what you think, I sick?' She replies, 'You're bright with potential . . . What about evening class?'

Then on Friday, eleven days later, she zooms up in a red MG. Hansie touches it, leaves the clam of his hand on the hood. Close up, her car's so shiny, too

5

swanky money. He reckons such-much rand notes could stack a truck, can't dream of driving again. She pulls out a black bag of stuff. 'A donation from generous people,' she says, 'collected by women of St George's Cathedral.' Hansie frowns. Her English is strange, a girl with grids on her teeth who says, 'I'm from Buckingham, England.'

The like-new caboodle spread on the ground – books, soap, pans, clothes – makes him point inside his shack: 'I likes dat lot, I picks dem up by my own.' Shakes his round head. She encourages, 'Go on, just try them.' Smiles, ignoring his waving no with his hands, pushes some gear on to his chest. He clutches the cache, withdraws into his dark shack. Is shocked how she's worked out his four-foot-six size. The black suit, shirts, jumpers, jeans just right.

So on Sunday he toffs up. The bridge-people butt, 'Ooh, now who you thinks you are? Maybe's you's gonna be our bridge MP!' A ouvrou pipes up, 'If your mommy see you now . . . You was a birth-baby crying for food, thin-thin, but big-round tummy. How many years Mommy gone? Maybe four, make you . . . me see . . . seventeen/eighteen . . . don't think you be more.' While other bridge-people snigger.

Hansie don't say nothing. Walks away, strides round the corner, grows to five feet tall up Adderley Street, makes a stop-off to smile at himself in the bronze façade of the Sun Intercontinental. He strolls through the Gardens with after-church dawdlers. Follows a smart Mommy, Daddy and two skipping kids through the Gardens, to the far end, to the National Gallery. Old Cape Dutch walls gleam white as they mount its steps. But they're stopped by ker-fuffle as they reach the entrance. The bouncing door-keeper roughshods a tramp, flings, 'You can't come in here drunk, dressed like muck.'

Hansie hears the Mommy's 'Do you have to?' and the doorkeeper's grumble, 'Madem, please. I know my job.' While Hansie fidgets, buttons his jacket, as the family pulls him inside. He's struck by the shine of the floor, the silence, the real look of pictures. Hansie's drawn to the Karoo. A bushveld painting. A pack of men trekking across Karoo's sand drifts, dotted with acacia trees. He leaves the gallery, muttering. Tjommelling about bleak desert landscapes.

In Monday to Saturday dawnings, Hansie dangles his legs from the flyover's gaping mouth, stares at the sea, where cargoed tankers are anchored. It makes waterless spaces kaleidoscope in his head. He throws off his clothes, stands still, alone. Crosses the Over-berg, sees little men loinclothed, padding across acres of sparse, grass-studded flats. Scans the dry distance of the Little Karoo, finds dun-coloured ostrich bathing in dust. Sun sparkles the sand, sprinkles his mind. His lips whitened by thirst, thinks, 'Water by bridge.' He tracks back, creeps down for drink, slogged, not got enough sleep, whispers, 'Next time, go slow-slow in sun.'

Hansie's mashed on Sunday, can't find his black suit, rumbles through his clutter, sits outside his shack, quietly keening. At twelve some bod shouts, 'You's want it. Come get it.' The bridge-people send shirt, pants, jacket sailing in catch-us-if-you-can. Hansie grips the ground, inside his head whirls, 'Fly – sun – desert.' They break up the game, saying, 'Voitog dopey, your mamma got you like dat.' Hansie runs round, grabs up his clothes, backs into his shack, swaps into his suit, dashes away.

Now young man thinking, 'Go smart.' Slows down Adderley Street. Ambles Government Avenue through the Gardens in the quiet afternoon heat. Circles neat flowerbeds of clashing purple and crimson gladioli that aroma December. Again, he picks a young family to follow. Drifts after them, slippers into the South African Museum. Hansie sees some rough brown-ochre stones, others shining as tiger-eye gems. Snow proteas climb Cedarburg mountains, pincushion proteas too, sun-yellow to poppy-red, scramble the Arniston coast. Hansie sticks these flower-pictures into his head.

Strides into the Natural Science section. Looks at the animals, zebra black and white pelts, striped heads of grey-bodied gemsbok, horns like swords. He returns to the impala, gets the turn of their heads, capers the corridors, skittish ready to hide.

Hears the family disgruntle.

The Mommy says, 'Let's avoid the next section. Uncivilized, showing people like that.'

'Like what? Primitives? Species?' The Daddy shakes his head hard. 'Kids must learn . . .'

'Nude . . . oh, why do I bother?' The Mommy grabs her kids' hands. 'Not with me, they won't. Disgusting, offensive display.'

The Daddy stands still, murmurs after her, 'Of blacks? What?'

She stomps on, yanking unhappy kids along.

And Hansie scratches his head, frowning. 'Why smart people be so ugly cross-cross?' He's not about to miss anything. Pads on. Discovers a chamber with glass cabinets of indigenous people: statues of proud Zulu warriors, Xhosa women weaving bright beads. San rock paintings, stick figures in green and rust, dressed only in hide; some straight, others bent, hunting. Hansie goes on to the wax figures of clay-coloured Bushmen people. Small men crouch, suck ostrich eggs or bore for roots near waterholes. Others coil bodies, ready to spear for the kill. Hansie gazes into their plastic black eyes. Traces a finger over his own flat cheekbones. Notices their tight, knotty hair. Hansie scratches his own kroeskop above his ears. Transfixed by their image, he sucks it under his skin. On weekdays, he bends a bow and whittles arrows. Practises his aim in glossy shop windows, sprints down the street. Regular passers-by don't stare any more. Think, 'Street-kid, high on glue.'

Hansie's a night-stalker, mounting his haunt on the flyover – above the unconscious bridge-people, hoping for the Southern Star to shine, a lucky sign. Good for veld hunting. The stalker finds beetle larvae for poison and dips his arrow. There's an odd aloe and nowhere to shelter. Dry sands burn his splayed feet. Trekking to the waterhole takes time, but it's shrunk to muddy brine. 'Must drink!' plays in his head. Midday and the sun shimmers the air, no animals there.

Stalker moves lightly, tracking impala, staring across the silence, over ruddy, bare earth. Moves away. Quickens. Sprints. Stops, spying a young buck, whose hide is shades of fawn. Reaches for his quiver. The buck's alarmed, sniffs, its paws ready to glide. Bounces away.

Closing his eyes, Stalker crouches on the hump. Feels a slither. Tenses and waits. Sees a monster gecko: skin scaly, back fins prickly, head the size of his fist, moving slowly. Stalker shuffles. Giant gecko barks. Freezes, blending into the yellow-brown clay dust. A blown dart pierces his head. The reptile twists. Shudders, dies. Is spiked on to a whittled twig, ready for feasting.

Almost sun-up and Hansie squats. Sears his meal on a nest of coals. Licks his lips. Rests, fades to sleep with its glow.

Wakes, works, sweeps through the week, impatient for Sunday. Bounds home from work Tuesday. Already bridge-people ring the galley. Swinging above it is his black suit straw-stuffed into a guy. He stands still some time, thinking, 'Julle blimsem, look again for brandy money. Won't find such luck. I not so dwars.' No use locking anything here.

The men tease, 'You wanna pay? How much you got? Where's it? Where you go in this blerrie get-up? You gonna be some street dominee?' They don't get an answer. A bloke pokes a stick in the fire. Torch the suit. Flame zips a pong, a spray of ash. Hansie don't cry, don't look, thinking no suit, no Sunday walking. Lies in his shack till St Mark's peals four, can't count time, but tells early-early morning by the gloom. Climbs up. Pulls off his clothes. Sits on fours, starkers in the brush, rubbing a black pebble.

Now a deer grazing, twitching his ears, his nose. Who knows what's lurking, though it's man he's most scared of. Lifts a hoof, takes off. Leaps on, on, on. Suddenly stops, drops his head on his forelegs, slinks off to sleep. Till traffic bumbles. Tugs honk their horns. Waking, licking his forelimbs. Shivering, checks, he's covered in short hairs like fawn. He twists his head, his cheek brushing a shoulder, thinks, 'Nobody see me.' Just the gulls squawk, starting for breakfast.

Hansie pops on his clothes, runs to work, collects

his cart and brush, rushes to press a snub nose against a mirrored shop front, giggles. No talking, just working, no looking at cars. Does his stretch of streets in short time. Itches to be clean.

Slipping down to the sea. Brushes shingle with sturdy-soled feet, picks up pebbles. Lopes to where waves crack the point, crosses rocks where blue periwinkles cling, stinging jellyfish wait for the incoming tide. Dips into the sea, gushes as cold bites his legs, wades, paddles in the bronze, snaking seaweed. Safe, no one else'll swim here. He drifts to a cove, scrambles on to the sands, shakes his hide, sprays water, nibbles a limb, pauses. Canters on all fours, climbs the bank and hill over the road, rests on a rock under clear sky, says, 'Dat Devil gone lazy.'

Frazzled by trekking, Hansie thinks dimly, 'Sleep Sunday.' Watches the sun boil the lip of the sea, till the waters turn green, ripple, settle like ink in the dusk, brood under black sky. Stars spark to the crickets' chime. The moon shines the leaves silver. His jumper and jeans dumped, the breeze licks his body stretched on the ground. Mind floating between sleep and awake, dreaming between being hunted and stalker, till sun breaks the morning, streaks the sky pink, touches his eyes. Still drowsy, he rises, stumbles on gravel, grazes a shank, drags on, dribbles blood unknowing, scrabbles Signal Hill's slopes. Hansie's struck by the sight. The flyover is a stalking hyena, jowled laughing, legs leaping to strike. Hansie flits faster. Fangs bared, barking, gallops back to its track.

Dives through the barbed-wire gap and strides the animal's rump. Moves tranced up the ridge to the screech of its jaws. Poises, body stiff, toes grip the ledge. Sucks in air loudly. Below, columns of people, tramping to work, stop, gawp. Point up, murmur. Call for help. Shout at him. Hansie vaguely hears cheers, sees arms stretch up to him. But the crowd's a heave of breathing, waiting.

Rubbing a black pebble, looks into the sun. Light braces his mind, slackens his muscles. Beyond shut eyes, he sees red and orange velvet. Is a Bushman hunting. An impala dancing. Bushman darting. Weaves red and orange inside his head, waits. Now a hyena. Screams, 'Jump!' and flies. Hyena leaping! Hyena hurtling, yawling, 'Eh-eh-eee!' Thuds on to the road. Lies limp, skin grey, hooves twisted. Hushed bridge-people ring him. He quivers his fingers, flutters his lids, gazes unfocused. Slow-slow, raises a limp fore-arm. The go-to-work onlookers sigh, murmur, expand into clapping, gabbling, laughing relief. Disperses.

The bridge-people straighten his limbs, cluck, 'What you's done? We fix you up,' lift him gently. A tail uncoils and slithers away. They carry him back to their row, fetch water, blanket and coax him into speaking. Hansie intones in a lilting voice they've never heard. They prod, 'Hansie?' Think he's speaking in tongues. Their eyes meet and tell he's gone to a place of his own. He hums, stares through them. They ask, 'You gotta name? Where's you goin?' Try, 'Wat is jou naam?', 'Waarheen gaan jy?', 'Ngubani igama lakho? Uyaphi?' He glazes a smile, his tongue clicks in Khoikhoi, 'I'm Oba, from the San kraal across the Kalahari.' They respond in anxious silence . . . can't interpret his words, but agree, 'He from dem people, go long-long time walkin.'

Now at night, they gather round the galley as he crouches, a troubadour with a bag full of tales, entranced by his strange sing-song words and grin, when he breaks, barks a shrill, cackling laugh. Hansie still doesn't drink, though when galley embers ashen, they all collapse together, huddle to sleep.

Sometimes in the glooming, Hansie cajoles them awake. Still drowsy, they drag from under the bridge, up through the wire, nose from where it flies into freeway, stop before it leaps into space. Hansie points to sea, stars, hills. Tells how they can cross mountains, lush valleys, over grass plains to desert.

Waiting for sunrise, they crouch hushed, eyes pricking the distance, wanting to see through the haze.

Maganda

Crista Ermiya

Inang said, 'Not every creature wearing human skin is a human being.'

Everyone called her Inang, which means 'mother', although in fact she was my grandmother. The Saturday morning before my ninth birthday she grasped my hand as we walked through the marshes, past the reservoirs and down Coppermill Lane to the market, where she was going to buy me a dress.

'What do you mean, Inang?' I had prompted, thinking she was about to tell me another story.

But instead of a story, Inang started to sing in a low voice to herself, one of those songs in her language that I couldn't understand, and so I quickly lost interest, caught up in a fantasy of the new dress. With covetous imagination, I had a vision of a little sailor outfit, with a blue-trimmed collar that would flap in a square at the back and tie in a neat little bow at the front, and frilly ankle socks, and burnished red shoes that had a strap across the front like tap dancer's shoes.

Inang would not be able to afford anything like that. She gazed down and asked if there was something I wanted in particular.

'No, Inang,' I said. But then, because I was still an eight-year-old girl after all, added, 'Something pretty.'

Inang smiled and patted my hand.

'Yes, of course. Something pretty, for my pretty girl.'

Inang was the only one who ever called me that. Every morning in the bathroom, Mum would hold my head in her hands and grip the sides of my face with a pinched movement of her thumb and index finger. She twisted my head from side to side over the sink, as if to examine better all defects from various angles. My ears hummed, while my head was held face down under the cold water. Mum would sing a strangled parody of an old song: your face will never be your fortune.

That Saturday, Inang bought me a red cotton dress from the market, chosen from an overstuffed plastic rack that had a yellow cardboard starburst with 'under £8' scrawled on in a thick black marker-pen. The dress had short puffed sleeves, a frilled edge at the hem and a low square neck with a shirred bodice. It was the prettiest dress I ever owned, before I grew old enough to make money and choose my own clothes. Mum wasn't one to dress me like a doll. Instead I would wear the cast-offs of various cousins, or drab acrylic polo-neck pullovers in bottle green, beige or navy that ribbed tight around my flat chest and wrists. Inconspicuous colours. Camouflage. Inang would not have wanted me to hide or disguise myself, but a few weeks after my ninth birthday she died. I was not allowed to go to the funeral, but I still had to wear black.

Twenty-one years later there is no one left with the power to forbid me to attend this funeral and I do so want to watch my mother's casket slide into the bleak gleam of the crematorium fire. I still have to wait; yes, I do. This being my mother, the whole process of disposing of the corpse is an anfractuous route of vigil, service, fire, wake. I am wearing a scarlet dress for the occasion. It makes the old women's heads turn in the pews and with one voice, like an amen, they tut-tut-tut as I clatter down the aisle in my four-inch-heeled courts the colour of the Devil.

'Sus-mary-osep!' an old woman blasphemes in a loud whisper, and her turquoise rosary beads fall to her feet.

'No respect, naman!' another crone exclaims in delighted agreement.

Once I reach my seat in the front pew, I turn my head to acknowledge the congregation, smile at the crones in the pews behind me. Their shudder is a Mexican wave that runs through the church, across the aisle.

I have always liked Ecclesiastes. The words from the pulpit drift over our heads and I nod in agreement: 'A time to weep, and a time to laugh. A time to mourn, and a time to dance.' I turn around once again to face the blaspheming old women. Their heads immediately slip away from mine to face front, face the priest. I turn back and can almost see their faces swivel again towards me, through the back of my head.

The priest reads from Revelation 22: 'Nothing accursed will be found there any more . . . They will look upon his face, and his name will be on their foreheads.'

Like the mark of Cain, but of course I don't say that out loud, merely stifle a giggle, holding up my freshly laundered handkerchief to my mouth like a widow at a murder trial.

More words at the crematorium. How tiresome ritual can be. I would have liked to choose the music myself, something in the vein of 'Disco Inferno', with its exhortation to combust. But Mum wanted Diana Ross and made her own arrangements with her cronies, so 'Disco Inferno' will have to wait for my own passing beyond the vale. Mum's coffin passes through the red velvet curtain to the sounds of 'Do You Know Where You're Going to?', and I need to raise my handkerchief to my face once more. One of the crones mistakes my mirth for grief and touches me compassionately on my forearm. I stiffen at the infraction and she pulls away.

'You are coming to the wake?' she says to me afterwards, the statement masquerading as a question.

'In a while,' I reply. 'I need some time alone first.'

Her wrinkled lips purse, so that her slack aged mouth looks like a lunar crater filled in with pink lipstick, but she nods. I exit into a waiting taxi.

I have already moved into the family home my mother left, an ex-council flat on the fourth floor of Hrothgar House, on the Kingsmead Estate in Clapton, between Homerton High Street and Daubeney Road. All the houses look the same: closed stairwells with new entryphones, each flat refurbished with identical brown varnished doors, red paint around the doors and windows of each floor, and new plastic white window-frames like Lego sections. From the balcony I can see Hackney Marshes in the near distance, with its football pitches and spiny shadows. When I was a child, everyone at school believed there was a bear on the marshes. Mum believed it too.

'Don't go there alone,' she'd tell me. 'The bear might get you.'

Then she'd pause.

'Although who knows?' she'd say. 'Maybe you're safe. Maybe the bear will be frightened of you and run away.' And she'd pinch my face, hard, and laugh.

'Dios Ko! What an ugly child.'

God's curse. Whether on her or on me was never made clear.

We are all born in sin.

On Saturday mornings or Sunday afternoons Inang would take my hand, and we'd go to the marshes and we'd walk and walk and walk. I was afraid of the bear, but Inang would shush me, and wipe the sweated fringe of hair from my forehead, tuck it behind my ears.

'There's no bear here. And even if there was, it's not the creatures who wear their fur on the outside that should scare you.' Her bony fingers gently brushed the thick down on my face.

Sometimes we would watch the football. Local boys mostly, some I recognized from school, too busy moving their feet around the small pitches and shouting to each other to call out names to me. Goalposts massed together on the marshes like white turbines in a wind farm. Mothers, stood at the sides to guard jackets and bags, would not look at me. Or they would look at me, without caring that I could see them looking at me. And sometimes a mother would look at me and smile, and that was worst of all.

'Say hello,' Inang would prompt.

And I'd say hello and wave. That should have been the woman's cue to say, 'What an adorable child' or 'What a lovely girl.' Occasionally, one of them was able to manage a 'How sweet' before turning back to the football. Sweet. Like a kitten or a poodle. At such times I wanted the bear to finally make its appearance, grim and greedy, and claim me for its own. But Inang would stroke my head, or hold my hand, and I would feel calm again and the mist that gathered in front of my eyes would clear.

On the days when there was no football or it was too cold to stay still, or on the days when there were too many people around who might look and point and cry out, on those days we would walk. Along the river path beside the marshes, over a bridge and back again, on to Walthamstow Marshes and the swans on the River Lea. A change from the grey pigeons that gathered on the estate and elsewhere, that painted the ground and crumbling brick walls off-white with their never-ending droppings. I would run ahead and brush my matted fingers over cow parsley and dock leaves. Inang would pick nettles sometimes and boil them up at home to brew a foul-tasting tea.

As we walked, Inang would tell me stories. From the islands, she said. Over seven thousand of them and each one different. Some had mountains and stretched so far you couldn't tell you were surrounded by ocean. Others had fields of rice, older than Jesus and cut into the hills like temples. On some islands, there were more turtles than people and at night the women would grow flippers and swim out into the sea with a shell on their back. On the islands, the women were always turning into something else.

'Like mermaids?' I'd ask. Mermaids were respectable. We read about them in stories at school.

'Pah.' Inang made a sound with her lips to dismiss the mermaids.

'Naked women,' she said, with her mouth turned down, 'who sing for fishing folk, or else cut off their tongues for the love of a man. No, child,' she'd say, 'that's not our women.' And she would tell me stories of women who drank the blood of their enemies. Manananggals, women who can separate their body from their legs, to fly up into other people's houses at night on the wings of a bat. An aswang, who has the ability to transform into a pig, a dog or a bird, and will steal a dead body and replace it with a wooden carving. Tikbalang, a half-human, half-four-footed creature who leads travellers astray by mimicking the voice or appearance of a close relative and calling to the travellers to follow them, into the woods or into the cavernous depths of mountains.

'To protect yourself,' Inang said, 'when you travel, you must walk with your clothes worn inside out, so they do not recognize you.'

'Ay nako, Inang!' Mum said, irritated, when I had explained to her why I had come home from school with my anorak turned inside out to show the orange lining. 'Stop filling her head with such nonsense.' And she pinched me, hard, on the fatty part of my left thigh. It doesn't matter about bruises, because you can't see them beneath the hair.

★

The wake is being held in a community hall in Manor Park, near the cemetery. Anyone who dies with an East London postcode ends up in this cemetery, loosely bordered by Ilford, Stratford, East Ham and Wanstead, that dead gash of land between London and Essex. I hadn't organized the hall. Like the funeral, this has been taken care of by Mum's cronies. I'm not certain 'wake' is the right term. When I get to the hall, the gathering seems more like an extended karaoke session fed with pancit noodles and chicken adobo, lots and lots of Coca-Cola and black coffee, and tuba, a strong spirit wine made from coconut trees that would have been sweet only on the day it was tapped from the tree. In the time it has taken to get to England the tuba has soured into bitterness.

All the songs being sung are either Diana Ross covers or numbers from musicals. When I arrive, the old woman who had dropped her rosary beads in church is doing a belting rendition of 'Somewhere over the Rainbow'. She even looks a little like Judy Garland as Dorothy, dark hair tied in plaits and slightly overweight, but with a lot more wrinkles and much darker skin. Judy Garland as shrivelled walnut.

Compassionate crone pops up at my elbow. She's that short.

'Eh, Maganda, where have you been?'

'I wanted to change into something more comfortable,' I tell her.

She looks at me. I am still wearing my scarlet dress.

I point to my feet. She looks down. I have swapped my high-heeled court shoes for a pair of eight-hole patent cherry-red Doc Martens boots. Just in case I want to go for a walk.

Her pink-lipsticked lips purse again, like they did in the church. I'm guessing it's a favourite expression of hers.

'Why don't I get you some tuba?' I ask her.

'I'm not drinking any alcohol until I've been up for my first song.'

I don't want to ask, but can't help myself.

'What are you going to sing?'

'"A Whole New World",' she says.

From the Disney version of *Aladdin*.

'It's a Pinoy classic,' she tells me.

It really isn't.

I ask if I can go up next. I'm warming to the idea of singing karaoke at my mother's wake. A time to dance. A time to laugh.

Compassionate crone immediately looks suspicious.

'What do you want to sing?' she asks me.

'Oh, I don't know,' I lie. 'A standard from *The Wizard of Oz*, perhaps.'

She clicks her tongue, making a noise like a gecko.

'We don't have "The Wicked Witch is Dead",' she tells me.

Am I really so transparent? Or is the gecko a mind-reader?

The rosary-dropping Judy Garland crone is coming to the end of her second number – 'Get Happy' – and everyone applauds. Another old woman takes to the stage, this time a shrivelled bag of bones doing a passable impersonation of Doris Day crossed with Yoda the Jedi. The hall is full of old Filipino women, women who you never see anywhere except at funerals and under the dryers at the hairdresser's. There are no men here. I can't even begin to care why that might be.

I decide to leave when Doris-Yoda starts singing 'Once I Had a Secret Love' from *Calamity Jane*. All my life I'd thought it would be fun to dance on my mother's grave. But that really only works when everyone else is weeping. I had underestimated the essentially cheerful nature of Tagalog ritual.

Compassionate crone grabs my arm.

'Where are you going?'

'No pancit is worth this,' I tell her, 'no matter how well cooked.'

And I stomp out in my cherry-red boots. The crone looks worried and calls out to me, but I start to run and can't hear what she is saying. I carry on run-ning until I get to the Romford Road. Then I slow down and walk for about five minutes, until there's a cab office ahead of me, tucked between a Chinese takeaway and a newsagent's that is now closed for the night. Above, Venus is low on the horizon, just starting to rise over the rooftops.

There are sweat stains on my scarlet dress from the running and they've seeped into the thin jacket I've worn over it, so there's no disguising them. So much for glamour. It's the hair, of course. So efficient at trapping body heat.

There's a woman with electric-blue eyeshadow behind the window of the cab office and she looks up, startled. Ah, yes. Years of painful electrolysis on my face and hands have shaved me into some semblance of a woman, but I'm still shaggier than Bigfoot under a full moon. I smile, and hope the cab controller will overlook the sweat-stained dress and Doc Martens and overhanging eyebrows.

'Can I help you, love?'

'Cab to Homerton please,' I say casually. As if I've just popped in from the takeaway next door. As if I've not just run away from a karaoke keening in honour of my dead mother, organized by a coven with a taste for musicals and Benedictine kitsch.

The bright-blue eyelids flicker but the controller's voice, to her credit, is steady.

'Fifteen minutes.' And she gestures to a plastic padded chair.

I sit down and flick through an ancient copy of *Hello!* magazine.

'Thank you,' I tell her. I'm still sweating.

The cab driver takes us the wrong way, and then, as we approach from an unnecessary direction, he refuses to go any further when he spots the old Hackney Hospital looming up in front of us on Homerton High Street. It's an odd building, I admit, especially with that full moon rising up behind the Victorian prison-workhouse silhouette of the lunatic block, but really, you can take superstition too far.

'But it's just another minute to Kingsmead,' I say.

'No.'

We haggle and he takes two quid off the fare. Then I get out of the car. The driver does a perfect, illegal U-turn and zooms off in the wrong direction.

The High Street is dead. I walk down Marsh Hill and Homerton Road and turn off into the estate. Hrothgar House is over on the other side, by Clapton Park, past Ironside, past Offa's Mead, Lindisfarne and Jarrow Way. I walk by various houses: Alfred, Aethelred, Aethelstan. It should only take me a few minutes to walk through Kingsmead to get back home to Hrothgar House. But, unaccountably, I take a wrong turn and here I am, outside Aethelred House again. And I didn't even drink the tuba.

There's a noise of bees swarming which makes no sense until I work out it's the wind in the guttering above me. I hadn't noticed the breeze was up when I got out of the cab, but I am definitely feeling it now. My back and under my arms dry cold where the wet stains are, and the sharp air that whips the fringe over my eyes makes my forehead feel like I've eaten an ice cream too fast. It's the sweat, of course; so efficient at lowering body temperature. My body. It all just works so damn perfect.

Unlike my brain, which is having difficulty focusing on basic compass directions. I'm walking through the estate in a straight line, except it can't be, because I'm back in front of Aethelred House and the bees are buzzing in the drainpipes again.

The estate looks different. Pre-refurbishment, more like how I remember it as a child, each section four storeys of brown brick and balcony, piss-stained open-access stairwells and overflowing oversized metal bins. Virtually every window and front door is fenced over with sinuous black metal railings, the window bars curving out like goldfish bags swollen with water. And then I hear the whisper behind me. I turn around but there's no one there. It's just the wind.

'Maganda.' Mum's voice. Mum's idea of a joke: my name means beautiful. The name of the first woman in Filipino creation, falling into the world from out of one half of a split bamboo stalk. I prefer to tell people my name is Maggie. Less alien. At the hospital they call me Shaggy Maggie.

'Maganda.' The second voice sounds like Inang's, whispery with age but sure and certain, exactly the way I imagine that I remember it.

I believe in the truth of all stories, but that doesn't mean I have to believe they're really true. I don't believe in these voices. But still, I turn around to see where they're coming from. Even though I know it's the wind. I turn back around, in time to see a movement in front of me, a flash of shadow, dark in the darkness, rounding the corner of Aethelred House, like a big cat or a small wolf. Someone's pet out for a late-night dump, I decide, certain that I'm not going to follow it for any reason. Instead I walk in a straight line, heading for Hrothgar House. I don't end up at Hrothgar House, and I don't end up back at Aethelred House either. Inexplicably, unreasonably, against all narrative causality, I am standing on the marshes, like I've taken one giant stride over Kingsmead and the River Lea in my red boots, and now there's nothing ahead of me but goalposts.

And in case you're wondering – this isn't a dream.

She's here, the likeness of my grandmother, hand up against a goalpost to steady herself, her other hand unseen behind the back of the likeness of my mother. Close to, their features lose focus, Seurat dots that only make sense from a distance or a photograph taken with a myopic lens. And they're standing too close to each other. So close you could believe their bodies are joined up, like a person with four legs.

Not every creature wearing human skin is a human being.

I pick up my feet to run away, but my boots squelch and pop in the marsh as mud sucks up to fill the new space. The two heads swivel soundlessly round on a stock-still torso until they face me.

'Maganda,' they call out, in unison, and a smile spreads over the two faces, wide, and then wider, too, too wide, until there is nothing but a single giant maw collapsing the two shapes, gaping across the breadth of the goal line. Its breath is cold and rank, with the stagnant smell of standing water and marshland. Crane flies and clouds of midges buzz from out of the enormous jaw and marsh water drips down the sides like drool.

It knows my name.

This isn't a dream.

But the shape of my name in the creature's mouth is decaying, along with its semblance of humanity, into one long howl of unrecognizable sound. Its pitch rises, over my head, above the goalposts, higher than the last remaining tower block in Clapton Park. All the dogs on the Kingsmead Estate start to bark. They howl in sympathy. The creature's cry rises still further until the frequency is so high I cannot hear it and my face aches on both sides, from my ears to my jaws and inside my teeth, down the sides of my shaven neck. A colony of bats, wings fluttering faster than swallows, zooms into the clouds of insects that are pouring out of the marsh-mouth. An owl swoops down low and rises back up with a small rodent clutched between its claws. The owl's feathers brush my face and I glimpse its victim, squirming. And do I remain statue-still during this howl? I do not. I squirm and curl like a question mark and hold my hands over my ears and hold my face and cross my arms over my body like a shield.

My jaws ache.

This is where I should wake up and find out, like Dorothy, that it's all a dream. Or suddenly notice that the bright object in the sky I thought was Venus appears to be getting brighter and larger and is, in fact, an asteroid about to impact. Some kind of deus ex machina. I am so beyond prayer in this lifetime, but right now my head hurts, my scarlet dress is covered in sweat, midges and marshland, and I am clicking my cherry-red boots like hell for home.

And then the scream stops.

When the scream stops, all the sounds it had been blocking out seep back: the whine of biting insects; the rattle of goalposts in the wind; the hum of night traffic on Homerton Road; a freight train from

Walthamstow, rumbling across the tracks over the marshes on its way to Liverpool Street; a jumbo jet descending on its flight path to Heathrow. Before me stands a creature, four-footed and knock-kneed in its alien landscape, slack jaw dripping saliva like teardrops.

To protect yourself, you must wear your clothes inside out so they do not recognize you. I take off my jacket. I even take off my dress, tugging it over my head. The wind ruffles my fur like stripes of grass stubble bending in a field. I turn the dress inside out, pull the sleeves of the jacket through the armholes and reclothe myself.

This displaced creature, with its hungry, homesick cry, closes its jaw and turns tail. It scampers off, across the marshes. I follow it with my eyes as far as I can in the dark. At a distance, I see it pause suddenly in front of a darker patch of movement in the night, something that causes it to veer off sharply in another direction. Exit, pursued by a bear.

All stories are true, somewhere.

I trudge across the marshes to the bridge that crosses over the River Lea to Daubeney Road. There are no giant strides. Instead I walk the unlit short-cut through Clapton Park back to Kingsmead and Hrothgar House. There's a snuffling animal, part bulldog, part not-even-the-mother-knows-what, left out for the night by its owner and burying a decomposing owl in the bushes next to the path. The dog pads over to me and nuzzles my hand. I pet it for a while and it follows me back to the estate.

This time, I find my way home.

Generations

Rowena Fan

Breathing is, perhaps, both one of the hardest and one of the easiest things a living creature has to do. Take the three generations of Woo women. Soon-to-be-grandmother Shen Woo was secretly tired of breathing. Soon-to-be-mother Ling Woo was breathing short, sharp, malicious breaths in order to contain the hideous pain inflicted on her lower body. Ella Woo-Nolan was about to take her first independent breath, stuck somewhere between the perineum and the edge of the universe. The comfort of the womb was taken away from her as she tore her mother in three places and glided into existence.

Welcome, little one.

The time was 6.43 a.m. Ella wore a suit of scaly skin and congealed blood, with a thick tuft of straight, black, Asian hair. A week later, it would be shaved off to prevent it from falling out in clumps. An old Woo family myth.

The new grandmother inspected the baby's genitals and sighed at the prospect of another female in the family. As a teenager she had been hit by a blind man's stick, a symbol of bad luck, and now, two daughters later, this screaming hybrid Anglo-Chinese granddaughter confirmed the fate of the family.

A woman, of course, can attract prosperity. She could marry a doctor or an accountant, a businessman or a professor. That would give the family something to boast about! They would worship him like a god, feeding him the best food whenever he visited. They would be hoping that some of his status would dribble down the family line.

Outside, on that gloomy Friday morning, the rain poured down relentlessly on a quiet town somewhere in northern England. It was a difficult time to be born. Local people were afraid of the 'others': those who spoke in different tongues; those who ate oily food with heads still attached and scraped every crevice for edible flesh; those who lived to work and never had any concept of leisure time; those little people with unmistakable jet-black, glossy heads. It was the 1980s and things were supposed to be so much easier for the new generation. Those who were born on this soil were automatically given passports, but they weren't *really* British.

Well, at least you will never know what it feels like to starve, little one.

At the family takeaway, the New Emperor, Man Woo, a roundish, bespectacled gentleman with smooth, dark skin, had been anticipating the phone call for hours. It arrived at 7.30 a.m. The terse voice of his wife confirmed that he had a granddaughter. He put down the phone and sighed at the prospect of another female, for women were the bane of his life.

Still, a life is a life. A life is a gift from Buddha. He plucked two incense sticks from a wooden vase and lit them on the steel hob. Standing squarely in front of his ancestors' shrines, he allowed the pungent, sweet jasmine scent to fill the small, cold back room. In his mind, he thanked Buddha for the girl's safe arrival. He would make congee, full of pork and thousand-year-old eggs, to help the little one grow big and strong. He would go to the chemist's the next morning to buy cod liver oil and give her small quantities so she would avoid arthritis in her old age. Was she pretty? Would she grow up to have soft, pale skin, unlike her grandfather? Dark skin was a sign of the uneducated.

His younger daughter, Mei, had woken and was now stumbling down the stairs after sleeping off the graveyard shift. Unlike her tall, lanky sister, Mei was round and chubby-faced, with thick ankles and wiry but heavy black hair. Her nose was flat and full, her eyes small and beady. She stood respectfully, watching her father's ritual and imagining the cramped living space being overrun by a child.

Mei was very similar to her father: calm and determined, simple and respectful of others. Her sister, Ling, was like her mother: hot-headed and passionate, stubborn and selfish. It was Mei who had insisted that the baby's life should be spared, despite the stigma that would be attached to a young, unmarried Chinese mother. It was she who would take her father to the hospital every week to use the dialysis machine for his failing kidneys. It was she who began to notice how her mother had started to overlook the simplest things, frequently forgetting to lock the doors and shut the till. Her worrying was endless. Someone had to worry. Someone had to take on the responsibility.

Who would the new baby take after, her grandmother or her grandfather? Her mother or her aunt?

The incense wafted under Man Woo's nose for a few moments, before they remembered the job at hand: they had huge sacks of potatoes to peel and cut into chips.

As time would have it, Ella grew quickly and steadily, with little margin for error. Fuelled by her grandfather's pork congee, by the age of twenty-four she towered over most of her family. She had her grandfather's sturdy stance and smooth, light-yellow skin. Everything else she took from her mother: she was lithe and had large, cartoonish light-brown eyes and permanently pursed, pink lips. Her long, dark hair was naturally straight with a slight kink towards the ends and a delicate sun-induced musky-brown highlight on her fringe.

She was the perfect Anglo-Chinese hybrid. It was

as if the harsh, jet-black features of the traditional Chinese person had been dipped into condensed milk, making her face creamy brownish yellow, with a sunny beam. People would stare at her, unsure what amalgam she was.

Since her Irish father had left before she was born, she grew up with all things Chinese. Boys would try to talk to her at secondary school, but her Oriental conscience would make her refrain from any type of shameful activity. She would run back to the take-away, ignoring as many of her peers as possible (head down, large strides) and curl up to watch *Neighbours* with a bowl of chicken feet dipped in soy. She remembered, too, how her grandmother had insisted she learn to play the piano because the Wongs' son had achieved his grade 8 certificate by the time he was fourteen. In return, she'd insisted on a new Sylvanian family toy every Saturday morning, so one of the adults would wake especially early and go with her to the largest toy store in Oldham to buy the figure of her choice. The other children were intensely jealous of her belongings. Her things always went missing at school. It was very true that she found it difficult to make friends.

In Ella's year at high school there were three Chinese girls. They sat together on the third wooden bench down from the school gates at lunchtime, with their glassy eyes and empty icy stares. The three trolls.

Two of them looked almost identical, with magnified, bespectacled eyes and stringy long black hair. The third girl was tall, at least five foot ten, with hairy, twig-like legs. She had tiny, cat-shaped eyes, with abnormally bad skin for a girl who had been fed good homemade soup by her parents. They were an insular club, doing everything together, refusing to partici- pate in games or answer questions at school. When- ever Ella passed, they would lean closer and whisper offensively, pointing, rolling their eyes and giggling, giggling, with vicious pace and malice.

Ling noticed Ella's lack of suitable friends. 'I see Chinese girl at your school. Be friend! Be nice! You never schmile!'

Ella considered this. It's not that she didn't want to smile. Internally, she smiled fifteen to thirty times a day, at the little things other people didn't notice. She smiled when an old lady managed to hold up the traffic, crossing the road with a devil-may-care swag- ger. She smiled when she saw happy couples who were unafraid of showing their affection, when being distant was an essential trait for an accomplished Chinese person. She enjoyed seeing people's doodles, especially at school, when she had to sit next to the class bully. She would sneak glances to see what could be going on in that oversized, over-solid skull. Most people would draw squares, rectangles and cubes, or start hexagonal stars in an attempt to look skilled.

The clever children, like herself, would cover the margins of their workbooks with circles, swirls and faces, and complex maps to buried treasure.

At the takeaway, where she spent every day of her life, she would sit on an uncomfortable woven chair in the corner as customers came in to be served. In her cheap reporter's notebook, she would draw their faces (always a round circle for the face and a stick for the body), and then write a quick description of who they were, where they were going and finally what their big dark secret was. She could never bring herself to write down her own.

She smiles now at those type of memories. It was a time when she accepted her family's values without question; when they were the core of everything; when relationships with the opposite sex were out of the question; when she could talk to white girls, but on no account act like any of them.

Her heart rate is beginning to climb. She is awaiting news. It's a Tuesday morning and the family are out for lunch. She has feigned a stomach bug – each member of the household had offered to stay with her and force-feed her black tea, but she declined. It's twelve now and realistically the postman should've come and gone – he probably has, but one can always hope. In a vain attempt to stop the butterflies in her stomach, she sits and counts the grains of leftover rice. One, two, three . . . it's hard to count rice when it is stuck together in clumps. The sound of footsteps can be heard in the distance, then the soft thud of paper hitting a brown woven welcome mat. It's here.

Ella walks as calmly as possible to her letter. She sits with it. She ponders all the possible outcomes. She doesn't even care. She really doesn't give a damn. She wants it to say yes. She wants it to say no. She doesn't know what she wants. People here need her. She needs to leave. Putting aside her hesitation, she opens the letter in one firm rip. Her trained eyes scan the document for key words like yes, pleased, accept, confirm, congratulations.

They are there, embedded in the letter. An acceptance from one of the best news agencies in the world, located somewhere in Arab lands. She had applied for the post with no belief in her ability as a journalism graduate to land the role; she was far too shy and retiring. She had stared at her brown loafers during the interview, the ones her mother forced her to wear because they were close enough to black, and no, new shoes were not necessary. She had most definitely been the only Chinese girl waiting in the reception. And now this! The possibility of something new and the escape she had always dreamed of.

Ling was a child of the 1970s. Arriving at the age of twelve and barely able to speak English, never mind having had the chance to dance to disco music, she found it difficult to blend into the background. People were fascinated by her. A group of girls would inspect her every now and then, looking at her dark irises and glossy black hair. They felt superior, as boys always preferred blondes, no matter how ugly their faces were.

She had friends, girls who would talk to her when they wanted some free food. Two in particular, Susan Sommers and Nicola Jones, would offer to walk home with her. They would ask her what she thought of their country; if she liked *Coronation Street*; if she really used to eat dogs and if she had to have an arranged marriage. When they reached the family takeaway, they would ask if they could come in and, sure enough, Shen would give them a portion of greasy chips, topped with mucus-thick gravy and enough salt to induce a heart attack. Ten minutes later, the girls had to be somewhere else, and would often leave without even a simple, 'I'll see you tomorrow.'

Ling would imagine she was still in Hong Kong, surrounded by her friends and her pet chickens, basking in better weather. Her mother had dragged the entire clan to England, supposedly for a better future. 'We don't have to like this country, or people. Just work hard!' Shen would often declare. 'Study! Work! Study!'

It was difficult when the English kids spoke so

quickly, with these thick accents – they didn't talk like how she had heard in black and white films. Those men wore long black coats with top hats and carried long canes. They were honourable and gentlemanly; they tipped their hats as they greeted people, always speaking perfectly: 'Hello, sir', 'Good morning, madam.' Women were ladies, with unimaginable grace and style. When Ling walked along the street, even though she took the same route to school every day, the same people still stared at her, as if she was suffering from bad karma. There were no charming men with top hats, calling her madam or opening doors. People scuffled a lot, and she was taught to keep important things out of her pockets in case they got stolen. She was spat at a few times, if that counted. People were peculiar in England.

She wondered if it was her lack of understanding of the language that was affecting her relationship with the natives, so she tried, tried, and struggled to master it. There was something embedded in her, though: she couldn't pronounce her t's properly or her r's. People would always smile, and take great pleasure in correcting her pronunciation. It was strange to her; here were people who couldn't speak a word of Chinese, not one bit, yet they were laughing at the fact that she could speak, but not quite pronounce, their language.

On Saturdays, when she helped all day at the takeaway, Mark Staley, a fat, hairy-bellied, balding taxi driver who lived two doors away, who never cooked for himself at the weekends, would take great pleasure in echoing Ling's 'plawn clackers'. He probably couldn't read, since he always ordered the same thing and by number, then asking for clarification. How incredible, thought Ling, that this man felt superior because he could pronounce words from a language he had been learning since birth. Surely it was the same as feeling superior because one knows how to breathe or to walk.

Ling hated the food she served to her customers, too. She could never understand why the young boys would spend their pocket money on a cup of gravy to drink. She hated the way they would buy a portion of chips, then throw the food at each other and occasionally the shop window. She thought it was so wasteful; her mother complained because she hated cleaning up.

As Ling continued to settle into England, working in the takeaway became as normal as washing her face. She saw the same kinds of people; occasionally, an interesting person would visit. There was a fat man, with a heavy Irish accent, shiny new twenty-pound notes in hand. He stank of cigarettes and beer, and was often unshaven with a slight cock eye. He also had four sons; three of them resembled their father, but the last boy, the youngest, had escaped the inauspicious gene pool and looked something like an Irish Richard Gere. And every Saturday he would come, with two of his friends, to buy chips and curry. He would look at Ling with his eerily transparent blue eyes and push a smile through his lips. Occasionally, he would touch her hand as she handed him the chips. If her father was watching, he would immediately start yelling obscenities at her, and she would recoil immediately and disappear through the beaded curtain. One day, walking home from school, he cornered her. He romanced her, bought her some food; he flattered her and convinced her that it was love. They consummated their relationship once, just once, but it was enough. He left for Ireland with no forwarding address.

Often, her father would sit his two daughters down in the small back room and pace from side to side, menacingly holding a garden bamboo in his thick hand. Then the lecture would begin: 'Engrand . . . not like Asia. We . . . no like Engrish. No Engrish boy! They no good!'

It was something Ling would spend many years reiterating to Ella. She had learned the hard way that falling in love and giving in to temptation were only for the weak. From the moment she had had her daughter, she knew Ella would be her only child and she would never fall in love again. There was no need.

She had Ella and she would spend her life moulding her into the ideal daughter. In her old age she would always be looked after – that is the benefit of producing a daughter. She is always her mother's possession.

Ling's father had always told her, in the style of a true armchair expert, that people have three events that shape their lives. The first was being born. The second was death. The third was something random, a decision, an action that would turn a mundane life into one worth living. She asked her father what his life-changing choice was and he replied, 'Winning the horse on Sunday. New Emperor! 33 to 1! Lotsa money!' Her mother would frown and concede that the most important event of her life was coming to England, leaving behind her wooden shack and all the people of her village. Ling's memory of her early life had grown sketchy, despite only spending four years in England, but she did remember her grandmother's browning, wrinkled old body, lying constantly in their bedroom. She would sit with her occasionally, fanning her face and talking to her, telling her about how the world was changing. Before they left Hong Kong, she remembers taking her to an old persons' home. It was long, airless, with three shadowy windows that illuminated the dust on the beds. Old people lay rigid on the grimy sheets, mouths gaping, drawing silent breaths and staring at the sky. People moments from death.

Ling's grandmother wasn't dead, even though she may have appeared so. Her granddaughter held her hand and wished people would listen to her opinion, but children have no rights. Her mother said, with steely eyes, that they could not take an old, useless woman with them to England. It would be a hard enough journey. She looked at her mother and, without bodily contact, left. There were random times that Ling would catch her mother shedding tears, always quietly and well concealed. She had failed in her duty as a daughter and the money she sent for her upkeep was compensation for the guilt. She hoped her daughter would not fail her. Ling would later realize having Ella was her life-changing moment. She would spend her life grooming her investment to be a good daughter, better than her mother was to her grandmother, and better than she had been. Disciplined. Faultless.

Ella knew this. She had known from a young age that she was allowed to achieve as long as she stayed within the clutches of her elders. She was an only daughter and her position in the family was always to protect those who had sacrificed for her. Her family had given so much to provide her with a hopeful future, so to leave them would only prove her selfishness, wouldn't it? She had her decision to make.

It's the most incredible type of loneliness that a child of two cultures feels. This person has been told from all sides to fit into the society they live in, like a dark inkblot trying to blend into cream vellum notepaper. It gets smudged, smothered, in order to lessen its impact. This lessening of their spirit, their soul, comes from the people they were born into and the people in the world around them. There are ones who tell them to be as true to their ancestry as possible, that there is a limit to how much they can integrate with the new world. Never forget who you are! Never forget to feed your family! Around you people are doing things your inbuilt guilt radar refuses to allow you to test. You are a self-restricting machine.

Two weeks before Grandad had died, he had bought a song thrush for Ella as a substitute for the dog she always wanted. It was matted brown, with cream patches. It had a long but sharp tail, and a proud, rounded breast that was covered in soft black freckles. Its new home was an iron cage, with chipped blue paint and rusty entrance, its floor covered with last month's *Sing Tao Daily*. Ella fed it bits of potato, cabbage and random leftovers before realizing birds ate grains and nuts. Occasionally, when she left the bird on her windowsill, it would tweet a few lines, high-pitched and delicate, while jerking its head side to side. She didn't know what the bird could see outside her small window, apart from a large oak tree and the grey muddy skies, and wished sometimes she could talk to the bird. It could never obey like a dog would; it was a thoughtless, thankless creature, leaving others guessing its pursuit of personal happiness. The bird stared into the darkening sky and wondered what it would be like to be free – it wasn't much of a world out there. But it was what he had as an aspiration.

When Ella was twelve she grew tired of watching the bird's restless demeanour. It had stopped singing so often. It would eat, flutter a little, sleep and do nothing else. Ella looked at the icy December cold outside, for it had begun to get frosty. She looked at her bird. She wanted to grant it freedom, for this must be the only thing that people want above love. But outside it was cold and the other birds had migrated south and nothing could possibly survive in that weather. The truth was, as much as she wanted it to be happy, she couldn't let go of her only pet.

It turned to spring, and Ella was thirteen. It was a warm, delightful afternoon and people were happy. People were smiling and interacting with each other. Even her grandparents were laughing. She thought then, with the beautiful orange sky, that perhaps it was time to let her bird go.

In her tiny bedroom, in the corner, her only window was gaping. Her mother had already been in, leaving her clean socks and knickers on the bed. She moved towards the blue metal cage to look at her pet, but noticed it was empty. It had gone. Ling appeared in the doorway. 'I let it go. Poor thing.'

It flew. It flew far and high, into corners that other birds of its kind had never seen before. And when it was ready, it would return to its nest, for it was never that far away from its consciousness.

Farewell, Love

Ahtzaz Hassan

I am mercy. I am eternal.

The old woman tears off a piece from a slice of organic wholemeal bread and tosses it at the growing mêlée of ducks, geese and swans gathering at the water's edge. The old man sits in his wheelchair and watches them, eyes occasionally moving from the Battle of Brown Bread to the old woman and back again. He watches as she tears off another piece and casts it further into the largish lake.

He listens as she scolds various individuals for their selfishness:

'Stop it, Donald! You've had plenty already. That was for Shah Jahan.'

'Gandhi, how many times must I tell you? Stop bullying Sikander!'

'Quickly, Jinnah! Before Bush puts trade embargo on your share!'

He watches from his wheelchair as she turns to him and starts to laugh at her own political witticisms, and a smile slowly forces itself across his face. The surreal concept: Disney's children stealing from Mughal emperors; adherents of passive resistance bullying would-be conquerors of the world; founders of a nation advised to be wary of oppressive US presidents. He shakes in amusement.

She has her favourite, of course – Sajjaad, a boisterous young swan with a single brown feather in his tail – and although she may occasionally raise her voice to him, she never quite manages to tell him off.

I walk around and past them to the weathered wooden bench some twenty yards away, where I am to meet Azrael. I am late. He is a stickler for timekeeping and won't be impressed.

As expected, he is already there. A quiet, constant presence. He sits bent forward, poring over a piece of paper, engrossed, his stick leaning against the bench by his left knee.

'Sorry, I'm late. You know how it is.'

I take a seat to his left. He looks up and continues to read.

'Y'know, I've decided I enjoy these times we get to work together.'

I lean back and look around as he continues to ponder over the paper.

On the other side of the lake, a young mother is lying on the grass with her six-month-old baby on her chest. She stretches her arms and pushes him into the clear blue sky as he dribbles his approval. A seagull flies over them, cuts across the lake and joins in the free-for-all bread give-away.

My companion lets out a sigh and leans back, staring straight ahead and focusing on nothing in particular. He looks up searchingly, as a plane passes overhead on its final approach to Heathrow. The vapour trail slowly fades. He looks back down at his knees.

'What troubles you, Azrael?'

He looks at me and passes me the paper.

Scribbled in peacock-blue ink . . .

A bloodshot moon,
clammy nights.
Mindless wonderances,
under soulless skies.
Time unrepentant,
yet hopeful sighs.
But what of hope,
when all else are lies.

'Fifteen years old,' he says. 'Only fifteen years old and no hope.'

I read it again and then one more time.

I lean back and watch the bird.

'No time to fulfil dreams. No time to have dreams.'

I fold the paper and hand it back.

'Suicide?'

He nods.

We sit in silence a while.

'It is not our place to question. Or judge.'

He says nothing.

'It is their fate, Azrael, their destiny. What is to be will be. But what they choose to do with their lives, that is their choice. It was all decided a long time ago. We cannot change what is written.'

He looks across the lake at the flying baby.

'We must do what we must do – nature of the job.'

He keeps watching the baby and it appears to lighten his mood.

'We are just the harbingers, we cannot be involved.'

The seagull dives down and catches the bread inches from a duck's mouth.

'How have you been?'

He shrugs.

'Why so upset about this child, Azrael?'

'I remember when he was born.'

'Hmm.'

The memory rushes through me – car crash, pregnant woman, Caesarean section. The child's time had started; his mother's was over. She had not wanted to leave the baby, she had cried for mercy, but I was just passing through, we cannot be involved – not my place to question, or judge. Azrael had done what he had to do and we had left.

The old woman is running out of bread. We watch

as she aims a large piece at a young swan, away from the reach of the others and low enough not to be intercepted mid-air.

'Do you remember them?'

He nods.

We remember everything. We never forget. That is our burden and our fate.

She places the last piece in the old man's Parkinson's-afflicted hand and urges him to throw it at the eagerly awaiting swan. He jerks his body – the offering flies through the air, one bounce on the bank and ends up in the water. It is accepted graciously. The old woman cheers and kisses the old man on the cheek. The disease may be taking his body but not his will.

I smile.

I remember when their story started, some sixty-odd years ago, in the small village of Dhok Duswandi, near Jhelum in India, now Pakistan. He used to sit on a mud wall near her house every morning and wait for her to go to the madressa. He would smile at her as she passed, and then throw dirt and mud on to her clean, pure clothes. 'Haramzada!' she would scream, and chase him around the village. The villagers knew they would be together; it was their destiny, they said. Then one day he took to throwing flowers at her and soon was caught and summoned before the elders. 'The boy has no shame. This type of behaviour has no place in Islam – either you marry her or stop this nonsense outright.' He wanted to marry her, he had said, if she would have him. She would. The families agreed to this joining and so it was arranged.

The years had brought them closer, their lives intertwined by the dance of time, their lives apart a distant memory now. She would send him to work in his fields after morning prayers with a soft 'Khuda hafiz – God be with you', public shows of affection being frowned upon. She would take him freshly made pakoras and samosas for lunch and they would sit under the banyan tree, her banyan tree, he said, and they would eat together and he would make her laugh and laugh and laugh, and they would be grateful to God for what they were given.

She believed in him when he chose to join the army and fight for their freedom. She sent him away to war in some distant place with a soft 'Khuda hafiz – God be with you' and brushed her hand against his chest, and he promised he would write to her every day. She would wait for his letters and, when one came, she would race over to the headmistress and ask her to read it. He would write to her of where he was, what he did every day and his company, and how he wanted to come home but he must first make the world safe for their children – of which there would be many once he returned. He never told her of the trains carrying back the thousands of dead, nor of the fields soaked in blood, nor how he sometimes didn't seem quite so sure whether freedom was actually worth the price being paid after all. Nor did he tell her that he doubted he would get back to her alive. He did tell her she was in his thoughts from his morning prayers until the night-time prayers, and thousands of miles away she would tell the head-mistress the same.

He finally returned two years later, bringing with him numerous treasures: saris made of Japanese silk, bangles of gold, children's clothes from Ing-laned. He was greeted with a quiet 'Assalaam-u-alaikum', and he could see she was crying.

They would have five children: two girls, a boy, a girl and another boy. There would be two miscar-riages before the first child was born and she would blame herself and lock herself away from him for days, refusing to eat anything. He would finally talk his way in and the two would sit for hours in huddled silence. It is not your fault, he would whisper to her, it is our destiny, our kismet – what must be will be. I love you, he would tell her repeatedly, I love you.

When Nasim – a soft, cool breeze in paradise, the first child – was born, their joy was contagious and all-consuming. For days he would sing and dance and be thankful to God and buy sweets for the whole village, and she would watch proudly as he showed her off to the world. She went with him when he took the baby to his father's grave and gave thanks.

He would be strict with his children and later his grandchildren, to teach them discipline, he said, but she knew. And so they knew. They would sit awake at night, watching their children sleep, and realize their place in life – it is only when you have found something worth dying for that you truly find something worth living for, he told her. He would promise her that he would protect them from the world until he could no longer breathe, and she knew he meant it.

It would turn out that he could not keep them all safe for ever.

The youngest son, Sajjaad, would be diagnosed with cancer of the gall bladder at the age of twenty-seven, four months before his wedding, and he would refuse to marry until he was fully cured. His fiancée would ask him why, but he would become annoyed and want to be left alone. But she would understand, and love him even more for it. He would never be cured. He would repeatedly beg forgiveness from his father, his brother and his sisters and he would ask his mother to hold him and rock him to sleep every night. She alone would know how scared he was. One night he would pass away quietly in his sleep, in a manner most unlike him. His brother would make the arrangements for the funeral and as people came to grieve and offer their condolences, his father would suddenly become an old man. He would sit quietly and listen to them recount stories of how boisterous and gregarious his son had been, how full of life. Too much life. While some aunties could be heard wailing from the other rooms, he would maintain a dignified silence and people would wonder why he never cried. But during the nights, when everybody had left and all was quiet, his wife could be seen holding him, and he would weep silent tears on her shoulder. I'm sorry, he would say repeatedly, and she would tell him ssshh and that she loved him.

It would take him a while, but with her help, he would eventually find his God again, and he would be thankful for what he had been given and he would finally be at peace. Even when he became ill and knew he wasn't going to get better.

He would be distressed upon discovering he had Parkinson's, but he would worry more about how it would affect her and he wouldn't tell her for six months, while she worried why he was upset with her. He wouldn't tell her at all that there was also something else wrong; the doctors didn't know what it was, but his liver was giving up, as were his kidneys. Slowly his body would desert him, until he could no longer move freely and only she could understand his new language. Only she could see the pain he had to endure each day, every day. Always the pain. But he would not want to part with her, and as each moment of life became harder and more expensive, he would cherish it even more. He would still try to make her laugh and laugh, and through the coughing fits he would still succeed, and she would become a young girl again, sitting under her banyan tree. But always the pain. She would pray for it to be taken away.

'Is it time yet?'

Azrael nods.

We rise and walk across.

She is standing a few yards away from him, looking out on to the lake, unaware of our presence, but he can see us. I look into his eyes and he understands.

'Ma?'

They always see their mother.

'It is time, Fazal-e-Rahmet.'

I take his face in my hands, gently kiss his forehead and take the pain away.

He turns his head towards his wife and says her name, 'Bibi'. She turns and smiles, and in that instant, standing with the sun behind her, he sees the eighteen-year-old farmer's wife who began his journey with him, as beautiful now as she was then, and he smiles back.

He turns to Azrael and nods. And Death does his job.

A tear rolls down his cheek, two tears.

'He was one of the good ones,' he says in her direction, as she continues feeding the swans.

We turn and walk away, and leave no footprints in the sand.

Mr Lee

Pauline Kam

There were many eccentric characters living in Liverpool's Chinatown during the 1960s. It was a thriving community based mainly around Nelson Street, crammed with bustling shops and small restaurants.

I first met Mr Lee at one such restaurant. It was a typically run family business where everyone knew everyone and would shout pleasantries and greetings as if they had not seen each other for months, rather than the week before.

The front was chock-full of tables. It was the New Year festivities and we were lucky to get a place. Families crowded together: mothers admonishing children and scrubbing food stains off faces with red napkins. Babies were rocked and the elderly fed, while all the time people chitter-chattered like noisy starlings, punctuating their talk with raucous bursts of laughter.

On my way to the small toilet in the yard, I was distracted by puffs of smoke billowing out like steam from train funnels from the kitchen's open windows. I peeped in, enticed by the wonderful smells. Bam! Bam! Cooks in stained aprons slammed cleavers into crispy pork crackling. Waitresses piled their trolleys with bamboo steamers and hot plates of sliced duck. Overhead, dead flies glued to brown paper strips twirled in the breeze, like ghastly decorative trophies.

In the back room, glimpsed through a half-open doorway, the lazy noon sun filtered through dusty blinds and cigarette smoke, highlighting the mah-jong players and giving the illusion of warmth. The elderly men laughed and swore and clashed their bricks.

Mr Lee came from the same village in China as my father, so he was considered family. He ambled through from the back, tucking a thick wad of notes into his wallet. This he placed in the inner pocket of his well-pressed suit. He was unusually tall and slightly stooped. I noticed his left leg dragged.

My father invited him to join us and we all squeezed up to make room. 'Eat up, eat up!' My mother exclaimed, thrusting food at him – sticky rice wrapped in vine leaves, barbecued spare ribs, pork buns. I eyed the last dim sum but she offered it to Mr Lee, the guest. He offered it back to my father and he pushed it back to Mr Lee. It was considered polite not to take the last piece. After much protestation, Mr Lee capitulated and, deftly picking up the dumpling with his chopsticks, he ceremoniously placed it on my plate.

'Here,' he said, smiling. 'Eat up, little one.' And everyone watched indulgently as, scarlet with embarrassment, I ate the treat. Instead of gulping it whole, as usual, I hid my greed behind delicate nibbles, savouring the succulent meat.

After the meal, the adults drank clear jasmine tea to refresh the palate. Mr Lee politely handed around the jar of toothpicks before taking one himself. He held one hand in front of his mouth as a shield while using the other hand to manipulate the stick. Even so, I caught a glimpse of gold-capped teeth. I was fascinated by such elegance.

Over the years, I learned a little more about him. He'd worked as a cook on the ships for the Blue Funnel Shipping Line, before marrying a Liverpool lass and settling down. After three years of struggling against public prejudice his wife left, unable to cope any longer with her family's censure. If mixed marriages were frowned upon in the 1940s, divorce was even more shameful. Mr Lee was damned by society either way. He never remarried, although he was considered a hard worker and therefore a good catch.

People talked about him. When he stayed at a boarding house, he kept the occupants awake by flashing his torch into the corners of the dormitory every hour. If he entered a strange building, he'd freeze at the door and scan inside until he was sure it was safe. It caused chaos in department stores.

He became a frequent visitor to our house. After my initial shyness, I was always by his side, waiting patiently until the adults had finished their conversation.

I never realized how poor we were, just that my mother shouted and cried when I pestered her for the toy cars and trains that the other children boasted about in school. One particular day after another scolding, I crept behind the sofa and eased my sore heart by picking at the mouse holes in the material.

I heard Mr Lee arrive but I was still too aggrieved to venture out, even when he called for me. The sofa moved as he sat down and I shuffled closer to the wall to make room. A few minutes later a bag of mixed sweets dropped on my head. It had my favourites: pineapple chunks.

Mr Lee listened as I poured out my woes. Instead of telling me toys were useless, as I'd expected, he showed me how to make windmills, boats and fortune-tellers out of paper. He mixed boiled rice and water to glue planes together. In return, I astonished him with my prowess at the times table and spelling 'a-p-p-l-e'.

He was astounded at my cleverness but insisted I remember my native tongue. 'Speak in Cantonese,' he said, 'or you'll forget who you are.'

I ignored his advice. I thought I knew best and, most importantly, I wanted to fit in. Foreign syllables crowded out my infant language. Now I struggle to understand my parents.

At that time though, I was content to perch on the table – cross-legged like a sticky Buddha – and relive Mr Lee's childhood through his tales.

Together, we meditated as the sun rose over the misty Guilin Mountains. I, too, tied glowing lanterns to kites and watched them soar across the night sky like shooting stars. During the Dragon Boat Festival, I leapt and slithered on muddy banks with the other urchins, all hoarse from screaming while urging on our favourite teams. When the snows fell, we celebrated the Winter Solstice. The whole village gorged on wonton soup, nine-layer cakes, toasted sesame seeds and savoury pork buns the size of spinning plates used by jugglers.

Then life changed.

Mr Lee seldom talked about the Japanese occupation but opened up when I told him how the other boys sometimes bullied me. 'I fled to Malaya during the night, straight into the arms of the invading Japanese. They were like locusts, stripping the land bare. People hid in the woods and starved when winter came. The babies had matchstick arms and legs, with swollen bellies. They were too weak even to cry properly. We knew that the army, stationed in the next village, had many animals: pigs and chickens stolen from the peasants. One of us would have to steal some food and make it look like they had escaped. Now, the penalty for stealing was harsh. A thief would have his or her hand chopped off. We decided to draw straws and the one who had the short straw would have to go.'

Mr Lee paused, as if he could still see the wartime scene again. 'I looked around. I could see everyone was scared but determined. The men were either old or lads like myself. I chose the short straw on purpose.'

He smiled. 'I was always quick with my eyes and hands. Ai-ya, we ate well that night.' He sucked his false front teeth appreciatively. 'Yet one time I was not quick enough. The youngsters were rounded up and forced to cook for the army. The Japanese had captured some British soldiers, who were made to work on the railways. They called them evil names and had them tied, beaten and starved. I think, deep down, they were frightened of the white men and believed swift, brutal treatment would break them.'

Secretly, each day, Mr Lee would sneak some rice from his meagre portion to the poor white men, but one afternoon he was caught and beaten until he resembled raw meat. 'I was not killed – I was too useful – but beaten savagely and paraded as an example to others. It was not personal; the guards were following orders. They knew the consequences of disobeying. That is why I am deaf in one ear. One leg healed badly, but I am alive and that is what counts. Even then, I did not regret. I was not beaten inside and that is important.'

He stretched out his hands, turning them to show his work-worn palms and scarred, tanned backs: badges of courage.

'So I should let them hit me?' I asked, puzzled.

Mr Lee laughed so much he started hiccuping and I ran for a glass of water.

'You accept what you cannot change,' he said, when he had recovered, 'but you do not let it kill your spirit. As for the boys, they follow one leader, and if you challenge his position and win, they will not bully you any more.'

He then taught me several moves that my parents would have disapproved of. When the older boys picked on me again, I stood up to the biggest and floored him. Mr Lee was right; they backed down and even asked if I wanted to join their gang.

Mr Lee was a popular player, gracious in defeat or victory. When it was my parents' turn to host the mah-jong evenings, I'd scuttle under the plastic table-cloth before the guests arrived. Nestling between the carved barley-twist legs, I was content to draw spit patterns in the worn lino with grubby fingers and lay claim to any stray coins that dropped from above. There was always quite a hoard around Mr Lee's chair.

I fell asleep during one of these marathon gambling sessions and woke up with a start. Woodbine smoke drifted in front of the coal fire. Occasionally, the embers would splutter and explode like mini fire-crackers, shooting hot cinders through the grate.

Mr Lee was speaking softly. The older generation were very superstitious and enjoyed telling ghost stories around the table, comfortably sipping rice wine from thimble-sized cups.

'Ai-ya, listen to this. After the war, I lied about my age and joined the shipping line. A handful of us had to cook for hundreds. On my first voyage, I felt drunk. My head whirled and throbbed and my stomach yo-yoed while we sweated in the steaming galley. After each shift, exhausted and bilious, I collapsed into a heavy sleep – no dreams, just blessed peace.

'One sweltering mid-afternoon, the older men invited me to play cards in the stores cupboard, but I craved sleep. I could always lose my wages in another break.

'I dozed on and off, my leg cramped and stiff. Suddenly, a child giggled.

'"Strange," I thought, "no child should be on board and certainly not down here. Perhaps it is an officer's child." And I looked up and saw with my very own eyes a little boy scamper past the bunks – a bright lad with round cheeks and eyes like berries. By the time I'd woken up properly and got to my feet, he had disappeared. I asked around, but no one else had seen this little boy. They laughed at me and said I must have dreamt it. When I asked the ship's main cook, he went very pale – which is difficult for a Chinese man. He made this sign.'

From under the table, I heard a collective gasp as Mr Lee demonstrated. I think it must have been a protective gesture to ward off evil. (My parents would not tell me afterwards, but berated me for listening.)

'The cook was reluctant to talk, but I persisted and he gave in. "Some years ago," he whispered, "there was a family travelling on board the ship: mother, father and son. He was a friendly child, always chatting to the sailors and showing them his wooden doll. Only one of the deck hands ignored him, but he was a surly man and didn't like anyone.

'"One stormy day, the little boy disappeared. His doll was found tangled up in ropes by the rails. The waves must have swept him overboard. The mother went mad with grief and ripped out whole handfuls of hair like this."'

Mr Lee suddenly wailed: an unearthly banshee wail that made me jump and shiver. I could almost see the poor woman clutching bloodied clumps.

'The cook leaned closer. I smelled garlic and rum on his breath. He said, "The deck hand was blamed for not tying up the ropes properly. He took to drink and eventually hanged himself. Since then, those who have seen this child running through the ship are cursed. Evil spirits are said to follow . . ." Here, the old chef paused, visibly quaking.

'"Yes," I urged, "follow what?"

'The cook gulped. I could barely hear his whisper. "Spirits follow them – even those who listen to this tale."'

The coals spat and crackled, shifting in a flurry of ash. A flame devil leered at me from the charred embers. Fiery claws lashed out. My heart stopped and I edged away from Mr Lee's chair. There was a horror-struck silence, broken only by a guffaw from Mr Lee. 'That was over twenty years ago and I am still waiting for the spirits to appear. Perhaps it is the English rain that is the bad thing, for it certainly punishes my aching leg!'

Everyone laughed and the delicious fear faded away in the refilling of glasses and cups.

Like his contemporaries, Mr Lee had a fund of stories about his rich and varied history, but these are the ones that stay in my heart. Isn't it strange how childhood memories are so vivid: clearer, indeed, than the blurred years that follow? The past sticks, like the rice glue.

I moved away and, as teenagers often do in their frantic desire to seek new experiences and meet different people, I eagerly shook off the past and quickly lost touch with my roots. What could the old possibly have to teach us?

A few years ago, my mother happened to mention

that Mr Lee had died. I had not seen or heard of him for a long time, but the news, so casually included with other snippets of gossip, gave me a pang of sorrow and a strange forlorn sense of something precious lost.

Perhaps, in these present days of commercialism, hatred and haste I finally appreciate the old values of honour, patience and courage. I'm not quite sure if it's as simple as that. I just know that, even now, I can taste that last dim sum and still feel warmed by Mr Lee's kindness and generosity of spirit.

Duck, Duck, Goose

Patrice Lawrence

Jackson was locked up. Locked up, man. His mum said if he took one step out the house she was going to beat him with an axe. Man, that boy was full of excuses. A few years ago, when his mum was working nights down the hospital, he would climb out his bedroom window to meet us. But he got to fifteen and all that fried chicken had set up home around his belly. He couldn't do escapology no more. And his mum stopped working nights when her sister went back to Jamaica.

I had plans for that night. Big plans. Two-man plans. And I had even sorted out precautions. For a couple of quid, Jane Tyzack would write a note from anyone's mum. The ones that I had in my pocket gave me and Jackson official permission to stay over at Heidi Barden's, signed Mrs Barden. (Heidi's mum couldn't write it herself, because she was visiting her sister in Brighton.) Heidi told me she was going to have her mate with her too. Like I said, big plans. And if anybody checked, our documentation was bang in order.

So I was sitting on the wall outside the flats, feeling

kind of let down, wondering if I should just forget it and go home. But my brother Lucan was back at our place, taking over my room. We'd end up in a fight. And Markie had been banged up again, so Mum wasn't in no happy mood either. Anyway, it was the first week of the summer holidays. Why should I go home?

And then I saw Connor. Me and Jackson have been hanging around together since before I can remember. Same primary school, same class, and his mum and my mum worked together for a bit before Jackson's mum got into fostering. It was funny. I didn't see my brothers from week to week, but at least I knew who they were. Jackson had a different crowd in his house every month. Jackson would come home from his paper round and find some strange kid pulling his best Levi's out the laundry basket. My brothers take drugs, rob shops and run a pirate radio station. But we respect each other's jeans.

Connor had been one of Jackson's 'brothers' for a couple of months, but I don't remember seeing him at Jackson's house. He was in and out of the area, and sometimes he would hang with us for a bit. He was a quiet one, but maybe with me and Jackson around he didn't have much of a chance to get a word in, even if he wanted to. And he was the only half-Turkish, half-Irish kid I knew, so that probably gave him enough to think about. But Connor was up for it. He said he hadn't had a bunk-up for three months. I nodded and hoped he didn't ask me my last time back.

Heidi lived about a mile away, in a small house near a late-night grocer. Heidi was sort of fattish and gingerish, and seemed welcoming. (When I was twelve, I found Markie's old *Charlie's Angels* poster and it kind of set my standards. But I'd given up being fussy a long time ago.) Heidi's mate Jeannie was skinnier and looked sort of Indian. Or Jewish. Or Greek. A bit like Connor really. And a bit like my brother Jonah. The girls were sitting on the doorstep, drinking Coke, when we got there. It looked like they had been playing at hairdressers. Heidi's hair was gelled and squished into two flat plaits running down the back of her head, like banks at the side of a railway. Jeannie's was sort of slicked and stuck down like one of those swimming caps they wear in the Olympics. They both looked terrifying.

'You look terrific,' I said.

Connor just stared. The girls stared back. They had been expecting Jackson. I had told Connor to buy a toothbrush on the way. He had forgotten to put it in his pocket and was holding it towards them like a microphone.

'Is that for me?' asked Jeannie sourly.

Connor made a sort of snuffling noise and looked vaguely down the street.

'Are you two gonna come in, then?' demanded Heidi.

Heidi and Jeannie were wearing these denim shorts. Which *were* short. Me and Connor bundled through the door after them.

Heidi's place was hot, man. Like someone had lit the cooker and left it on all night. The curtains were drawn. It smelt like they had never been opened. I think Heidi's mum worried that her sofa might fade or something. Connor asked about the garden at the back, but Heidi said that it was all overgrown and her mum only used it to empty the kitten's litter tray. Jeannie grabbed the sofa, and me and Connor perched on the floor, trying to forget about the bits sticking to our trousers. Heidi fetched some of those Toytown tins of lager and put on some soft reggae-type music. Jonah used to play that stuff at the radio station before he converted to rave.

We all got talking. Well, I talked. The girls sipped their beer and listened. Suddenly, Heidi sat back and sighed.

'God, it's hot in here,' she said. 'Why don't you take off your shirts?'

'Just open a window,' said Connor. Was he stupid? Or just not as desperate as me?

'If we open a window,' said Heidi smoothly, 'we can't play the music loud.'

'Are you shy?' Jeannie was looking at us with this

kind of sneer on her face. I was glad that she was Connor's. She was sharp-looking, man, with these ridgy type of knees that could grate a guy's ribs.

'Fresh air's healthy.' Connor headed towards the window.

I grabbed him and pulled him out of the door.

'What are you playing at?' Connor was vexed. 'Pulling me around like some kind of pussy.'

'No, man. What are you playing at?'

Connor waggled his armpit towards me.

'My shirt's all stuck to me. And it stinks in there. What's wrong with opening the window?'

I took a deep breath. Like I said, these were two-man plans, and if I came down too heavy, Connor would split. And I couldn't take on both them girls by myself. No way.

'Connor,' I said. My voice sounded like the maths teacher when she was cutting up circles on the black-board. I never understood what she was doing, but I didn't feel bad for not understanding. 'Man, it needs to be hot so that they can make their excuses.'

'For what?'

I sighed in my head. But then, I suppose, Connor had been moving from house to house since he was six. He never did nothing without asking questions.

'They need excuses to take their tops off. We go first, and then . . . well, you know. We talked about it on the way down.'

'But you didn't say I was getting the bony, moany one.'

'You want the fat ginger one? Fine! Fine! Now, let's take off our shirts out here and get back inside before we don't get nothing at all.'

The girls were chatting when we returned. They stopped when they saw us.

'Feeling a bit faint, were you?' asked Jeannie.

I couldn't look Connor in the eye. If I did, she would be mine.

I don't know what I expected to happen next. Maybe the girls would take off their tops and we would play strip poker. Or strip snap would do. Or Heidi would lead me upstairs and, well . . . Well, that isn't what happened. There was a knock at the door.

'Your mum?' I tried to sound cool, but Heidi's mum was famous for beating up a copper when she was eight months pregnant. I didn't fancy my chances against her, even if she did get round to reading the note Jane Tyzack had written on her behalf.

'Mum doesn't knock at her own door.' She went to the door. She sounded a bit nervous.

'Didn't want to meet Heidi's mum, then?' asked Jeannie, with this annoying smile.

Connor was about to answer and he had this rough frown on his face. I was ready to jump in between them, but didn't get a chance. A mad, loud scream came from the hallway. We all stared at each other. Even Jeannie looked as if she was about to wet herself. This wasn't a girl's scream, or a scared scream. This was the scream that a killer makes before he drills through your heart. For one split second I thought about jumping out the sitting-room window and running down the street. But it was too late.

There were two of them, in balaclavas, with bats and sticks. Only two of them, but it was like they could fill Wembley. Me and Connor sat there stunned. I think Jeannie thought we would defend her honour, but I would have gladly offered her up if it meant we would be saved. With her sour face and sharp elbows, we could have used her for a weapon. But they ordered her out the room and she scuttled away, looking scornfully back at us.

'Right, you little bastards! Get on the floor! Face down!' The biggest one pointed to the floor with his bat, just in case we got lost on the way down.

'What the fuck . . .' Connor started to protest.

'Did I say talk, Paki? Did I say talk?'

This was the other one, who was a bit fatter and had a creepy, slightly familiar voice. He reached to grab Connor by the collar. Then he noticed that Connor wasn't wearing no shirt. He didn't look up for no skin-to-skin contact. He lifted his bat above Connor's head.

Connor carried on. 'And I ain't no Pak –'

The bat came down hard. I closed my eyes and heard the thwack.

'You cracked the frame, man!' said the tall one, sounding a bit worried.

I opened my eyes. Connor was in one piece, but the sofa looked all wonky.

'We'll blame it on the Paki,' said the fat one.

This time Connor stayed quiet. They tied our hands behind our backs with this washing-line-type stuff and jammed rags in our mouths. They didn't blind-fold us. But me and Connor wouldn't look at each other. You don't want to see your mate scared shitless, because that way you don't have to lie about it after-wards. Where was Heidi? Had she gone to phone the Old Bill?

Me and Connor were marched out the back door and into the garden. It didn't smell of cat shit. It smelt of smoke. Heidi only had a bit of a garden. The rest of it was shared with a couple of other houses and some flats. There was a bonfire.

'Hang on, mate,' said the fat one. 'I left the petrol in the car.'

He trotted back to the house. Me and Connor were pushed towards the fire. They had it all prepared – two posts sticking out of the ground and a pile of sticks beside. All they had to do was tie us to the poles, scatter the sticks, a splash of petrol, a stray spark. I knew the scene well. I had helped three of my cousin's Sindy dolls go that way in my *Temple of Doom* phase. But this weren't no plastic that was going to be burnt. My mouth was gagged. There was only one way for my dinner to come out.

The fat one came back waving the petrol can. They tied us tight, tight, man, facing the fire. We could hear them behind us, singing like we were their football team.

'What are we going to do? Burn 'em! Burn 'em! What are we going to do? Burn 'em on the fire!'

'Which one are we going to do first?' hissed the fat one.

'Eenie, meanie, minie, moe,' sang the tall one, 'catch a Paki by the toe. The Paki. Do the Paki first.'

The fat one threw some sticks around Connor and splattered on petrol.

'Anything to say, Paki?'

The tall one undid Connor's gag and pushed his navy, woollen face right up to Connor's. Connor shrieked back, not an angry shriek, but a kind of desperate one.

'I ain't no Paki! I'm Irish!' He turned and looked me full in the face. 'Him, his brother's black! Proper black!'

Even without a gag, the words couldn't have come out of me. I stared back at Connor – and then one cool thought went through my mind. Peter denied Jesus three times and got the keys to heaven. A shit-scared, skinny white kid from Hackney ain't gonna trouble God's time.

'True?' asked the fat one. 'Your brother's a Paki too?'

I shook my head like it would break off my neck. God might forgive me. But would Jonah?

'Looks like you're lying,' growled the tall one.

He took a lighter out of his pocket. It was a red lighter and you knew that he had got that one and another nine cheap at Kingsland Waste. He flicked it on. Then he let the flame die.

'They know we can't do anything here. There's too many witnesses. I think we should take them for a ride instead.'

'Yeah, ride,' echoed the fat one. I could feel him rubbing his hands in excitement. 'What about Whipps Cross? If anybody hears the screaming, they'll think it's coming from the hospital.'

They untied us from the poles and marched us back through the house. No sign of Heidi. Or the Old Bill. An ancient Austin Marina was parked at the front of the house, with its boot gaping open. The fat one grabbed the back of my neck and pushed me down so my nose was on the rim of the garden wall. I once saw Jackson's dad down a can of Tennent's Super in one and scrunch up the can. That was my body, all pushed together and empty. Connor's nose was parked next to mine. The fat one leant down until his face was between ours.

'Good luck,' he whispered.

I caught a glimpse of his ginger hair as he stood up. Then there was silence. And the silence went on. And on, until a car engine started up.

I could hear some poor sod buggering up *Family Fortunes* on a neighbour's telly. Uh-aaaah! I could hear buses creak to a halt at the stop at the end of the road and the conductor ringing for the driver to pull off. I could hear Connor's heavy breathing next to mine. We looked around. The road was empty. Connor jumped up, grabbing me by both shoulders, shaking me like wet washing.

'You denied your brother!' he screamed. 'You denied your fucking brother!'

I still had my gag on, so I couldn't answer back. But he'd denied his own father! Irish, he said. Irish! Maybe it wasn't the same. I had shared a room with Jonah since I was three. He had taught me how to steal lead from the Mission roof and where to get the best prices. But Connor, well, I suppose it was an accident that his dad was Turkish. On another day, he might be African or Greek. Connor's mum wasn't a racist.

I undid my gag – just an old piece of sweaty-looking rag – and threw it into the gutter. Without saying anything, we went back into the house. The girls had reappeared in the front room. The music was much louder than before. Heidi was holding this spindly, crooked spliff.

I tried to smile at her. 'Your brother's still got the Marina, then?'

She didn't say nothing, just handed Connor the spliff. I reached for my rucksack and went to the bathroom to change.

That should have been it. You talk to your mates about how you know a girl's up for it and when she really isn't. When you go to a bird's house and you get kidnapped and nearly cremated, it's odds on that she doesn't want anything to do with you. But me and Connor – we went back into the house. We were fifteen. The girls were wearing hotpants. It wasn't just our feet leading the way.

Round about midnight, things started to chill out again.

'We're out of beer and Rizlas,' announced Heidi.

Things weren't chilled enough to survive without either. So the four of us set out for the late-night store. We got the skins, but the guy would only sell cans to regulars after hours. And since none of us looked eighteen, there was no chance. Connor could have given it a go, but he wasn't in no mood to cooperate. As we were standing outside the store, working on our alcohol dilemma, a green car pulled up beside us. Jeannie and Heidi had changed out of their hotpants, so it couldn't have been that. And anyway, there was a couple of brasses old enough to be Heidi's granny glaring into minicabs at the end of the street. Maybe the geezers were looking to flog a car stereo. I turned to Heidi. She was bricking it, man.

'Uncle Benny,' she squeaked, and went running off down the road, with Jeannie close behind.

Uncle Benny got out the car. He was a short, mean-looking geezer with slicked-back hair and a pissed-off expression. And then the guy sitting next to him got out the car. He was a tall, mean-looking geezer with a wide chest and a pissed-off look. He was also carrying a jemmy. I felt the breeze as Connor went hacking past me, with me overtaking him, like Roadrunner on speed.

It was a sick chase really. It wasn't our manor, so we only had a hazy idea of what estates to cut through and what were dead ends. But every time we came to a corner, we knew that Uncle Benny and his jemmy friend would be there. We scaled walls, trampled gardens, scraped over fences and skidded along pathways, which in some strange, lopsided circle led us back to Heidi's road.

Heidi was waiting there with my rucksack.

'Where the fuck have you been?' She pushed the bag into my arms and hurried back towards her house.

'Getting away from your psychopathic family!' I yelled after her. What right did she have to be pissed off? All we needed was to be raped by hillbillies to end a perfect night.

Heidi stopped and turned back. She was standing underneath a dodgy streetlight, the bulb going on and off like it was having a tantrum.

'Uncle Benny's at home. He's been there for ages. I told him that me and Jeannie had just gone out for more Coke and we met you two there.' She stared at me, with that light blinking on and off her face. 'My uncle and my brother are waiting for me at home. I would hate them to come out looking. Have a good night.'

I wanted to hug her. But she would think that I was still gunning for a snog. Sometimes even a gobby sod like me doesn't know what to say.

I couldn't go home. My mum didn't expect me. She would let me in, but I didn't want to explain. Lucan had probably nabbed my bed anyway. Connor's foster mum locked the door at midnight. We had nowhere to go.

We started wandering back to my area. Maybe my aunt would let us in.

'What's that?' It was the first words Connor had said to me in over an hour. 'Across the road there.'

'Doctor's. They alarm it straight to the Old Bill because of all the junkies breaking in and nicking the prescriptions. I think it was the doctor there who . . .'

'No, next to it. Behind that wall.'

We could just about make out a sheet of corrugated metal on wooden stilts.

'What do you think I am? Fuckin' Zebedee or something?' I started to walk away.

'I ain't spending the night on the road.'

Connor eyed the opponent. He's tall and slim. A bit like those guys they have waving their arms around in the front of *Top of the Pops*. Me, I'm short. Wall-scaling isn't my thing. Not unless I've got a car stereo tucked under my arm to boost my motivation. Connor took one big run, a foot on the wall and he was on top with his hand stretched out to me. I took a deep breath, hoping the extra air would swell up my sparse muscles. I launched myself towards the wall, closing my eyes as I hit the concrete. Luckily Connor's were open, and he grabbed my hand and pulled me on top. We landed on the other side together.

It wasn't the plan, spending the night trying to get comfortable on polythene and gravel, under nothing but a piece of tin. But it wasn't cold. It didn't rain. And we had plenty of time to try and sort out the details, cause we knew that when we told the tale to Jackson, somehow we had to come out looking good.

Diving in Tokyo

Aoi Matsushima

Building a diving pool in a department store in the middle of Tokyo was a mad idea; no one believed it would happen. But this was 1989, a time when anything was possible, and when it actually happened, the media swarmed all over it.

'There's a new guy in the diving section,' Kyoko said, coming back to our small office, which could barely fit two desks and a filing cabinet. 'He's kind of cute, and I think he'll be a real help to you, Mai, because he's amazingly . . .'

Just then, the phone rang, so I had to answer. 'Press office! May I help you?'

It was from a journalist researching an article on 'Retail Stores of 1989'. In the meantime, Kyoko took another call from a diving magazine. And as soon as I put down the receiver, the phone immediately rang once more . . . Nearly an hour later, we could talk to each other again.

'So how did the TV shoot go?' I asked.

'Fine,' Kyoko said, cutting out the magazine pages in which products from our store were featured. 'This new guy helped me to clear a space for the camera. He's very supportive . . . Where are the Post-its?'

'Here. Which issue is that magazine?'

'October. Anyway, this guy Naoki is pretty impressive. He can speak a lot of languages. It'll be a great help for you, won't it? The sales assistants will stop calling you whenever a foreigner comes in.'

'Maybe,' I said, with mixed feelings about having another language specialist in the store. I had been the only English-speaker, which made me somewhat unique.

'Which languages does he speak?'

'Mandarin, Cantonese . . .'

'Oh, so he speaks Chinese. That's great,' I said, secretly relieved . . . no competition.

'He studied at the University of Beijing, he said. And he can speak English, French, Spanish . . .'

'Has he lived in Europe as well?'

'I don't know. He said something else . . . Oh, Arabic.'

'Arabic?'

'Yeah, amazing, isn't it?'

'How did he manage that?'

'Guess he's from a pretty wealthy family, a diplomat's son or something.'

'Then why is he working as a sales assistant?'

'I didn't have time to ask him. He was wearing a trainee badge, so maybe he's doing work experience.

But he's not arrogant, he's very friendly. You'll like him, Mai.'

Then the phone started to ring, putting an end to our gossip.

Two weeks later, I met this Naoki in person. He came to our office with a bunch of new brochures about diving lessons for PR use. It was Kyoko's day off, so I was alone in the office.

'So, are you the new guy in the diving section?' I said, looking at his trainee badge.

'Yes.' He smiled. I knew what Kyoko meant by 'kind of cute'. He wasn't particularly good-looking; he was skinny and pale, wearing glasses, not like his tanned and well-built colleagues in sports. But he had a smile to light up the room, and it made him look like a little boy full of curiosity, as he checked out our tiny PR office.

'Do you have the international PADI licence?' I asked him, looking at the diving brochure.

'Not yet. But I've done several trial dives in Australia,' he said, looking at the piles of magazines on my desk. 'I'd love to do that again. It was absolutely beautiful, with amazing fish. I even saw a shark. Do you dive?'

'No.'

'Not even a trial one? It's fun.'

'No, but I feel like I have, after talking about our diving pool so much to journalists.'

He turned to me and smiled. 'The publicity's great. Do you do the PR for the entire store?'

'No, no, just for this new wing. The main PR office is at headquarters. We set up this small branch office because there were so many inquiries about the new wing, and the target market is too young for the old men at headquarters.'

'It looks like a cool job.'

'It's not as glamorous as it sounds. It's a bit like a call centre.'

'What are these on the shelves? New products?'

'Yes, they are for promotion.'

'I can bring new sports products here for publicity!'

'Thanks, that'll be a great help,' I said. Kyoko was right, he seemed to be very cooperative. 'And I've heard that you speak some languages?'

'Yes.' His eyes lit up. 'I can speak Mandarin, Cantonese, English, French, Spanish, Brazilian Portuguese, a little bit of Russian, Hungarian and some Arabic.'

He said all this within a breath, and it took a while for me to digest the information. 'That's amazing,' I said, after a pause. 'Do you speak as many languages as Schliemann?'

'Who is that?'

'Never mind.'

I couldn't believe him as easily as Kyoko did. What he didn't know was that I had majored in languages – English and French – and knew what it takes to speak several languages, especially languages with such different structures as Arabic and Chinese. But Naoki was smiling, looking straight into my eyes, and didn't seem like the kind of guy who lied. Surely 'Brazilian Portuguese' or 'Hungarian' was too specific to be a lie. Maybe he could speak some languages fluently and knew a few phrases in others. He wanted to boast because he was new to the company. I was tempted to speak to him in English to test his ability, but the phone rang again. So I was back to work, and he returned to his floor.

At lunchtime in the canteen, I happened to queue behind another sales assistant from the sports section. I knew him quite well, because we had joined the company at the same time four years earlier, so I asked him casually about this new trainee's language ability.

'Oh, you heard about it?' he said. 'Isn't it amazing? At his age!'

If the people from his own section said so, I had to believe it. 'How old is he? He looks quite young.'

'Twenty or twenty-one, something like that.'

'But I heard he graduated from the University of Beijing. He couldn't be that young.'

'He skipped some grades when he lived in the USA.'

'He lived in the USA?'

'So I've heard.'

I didn't say anything further and moved on to order pasta. But it was strange to hear that Naoki had once lived in the USA. I myself had lived in London in my childhood and I could usually tell the people who had been brought up in Western countries from their mannerisms or body language. We could sniff each other out, like dogs. But I didn't notice any signs from Naoki. Or had he lost them while he lived in China?

A few days later, I heard the same story from Mrs Akao, who was in charge of training recruits. No one would have the guts to tell her a lie.

'Isn't it a shame he's working on the sales floor?' Mrs Akao shook her head. 'He should be transferred somewhere he can use his languages.'

But his immediate boss, Mr Tanabe, didn't seem to know about his skills. I'd seen him treating Naoki just as roughly as he would any trainee.

'He's a son of one of the major shareholders,' Kyoko explained to me a week later, after another photo shoot at the diving pool. 'He didn't even know it himself, until someone else told him. His father wanted him to start a career just like anybody else and he asked Mr Tanabe to take him under his wing as a trainee.'

Kyoko had more opportunities to meet Naoki, as

she loved watching over TV shoots to get out of our little office, while I handled press interviews with the store manager. She had been working as a sales assistant since finishing high school and hated desk-work. If she didn't suffer from back pain she would never have left the sales floor. For her, the only good thing about PR was being able to chat with people.

Every time she came back from the diving section, she told me how helpful Naoki had been: he had the new merchandise and brochures ready for the media; he assisted them by carrying camera equipment, being friendly and attentive. He was still a trainee, so he wasn't interviewed like the senior sales manager or the diving instructor. But he was definitely playing a key role in the PR work. Since he had joined, the display shelf in the press room had never run out of diving-pool brochures or other new products. Occasionally he even dropped by during his tea break just to say hi to us. Yes, he was a nice boy.

'He's always learning something,' said Kyoko, as if she was talking about her little brother. 'He's taking a correspondence course for accounting. He says he likes getting qualifications, and he's saving money to take his diving licence next.'

The only time I did PR for the diving pool was when foreign journalists came. It didn't matter which country they were from, what language they spoke –

I was the international PR officer and I loved it. The 1980s provided foreign journalists with no shortage of materials for articles on the 'eccentricity' of the Japanese, and the diving pool was one of them, attracting headlines like 'A Compact Pool in Tokyo' or 'Instant Diving'.

One day a journalist from Hong Kong wanted to see the pool. I didn't know how good his English or Japanese was, as I had previously communicated with him only by fax. But Kyoko reassured me that Naoki would assist me, and she had warned him in advance.

I waited for the journalist at the entrance of the department store, but he was late and I was getting anxious. Soon the person on the information desk came to me.

'There's been a call from the diving counter,' she said. 'The Chinese journalist is already there.'

'Thanks,' I said with relief, and rushed to the diving section. I was hoping that Naoki was being attentive and showing the pool to the journalist. But when I got there, I found the journalist standing in the corner, like a lost child. I couldn't see Naoki anywhere and there was only a part-time sales assistant at the counter.

Luckily Mr Lee, the journalist, was fluent in English. He was one of those people in Hong Kong who had spent most of his life in England and he was pleased with my English accent. His worried face cheered as I guided him to the diving pool.

'Do you dive, Mr Lee?'

'No, unfortunately.'

I was secretly relieved, because he probably wouldn't ask me anything too technical. Even so, I looked for Naoki from the corner of my eyes, in case Mr Lee wanted me to explain something I didn't know about.

'The pool is four metres deep,' I said. 'We built it with the image of sea in mind. See the motif of waves on the wall?'

'Yes, it's pretty. But isn't the pool too small?'

It was, actually. But I kept smiling. 'Well, it's big enough for the initial lessons. We also arrange lessons in the sea for those who want to take the licence.'

'Where do Japanese people dive? Okinawa?'

'The islands of Okinawa are beautiful, but there are places nearer Tokyo. You can get to Atami in less than an hour.'

'Isn't it the place famous for hot springs?'

'There are pretty dynamic diving spots as well.'

I was hoping that he wouldn't ask me any more about Atami, because I'd never been there. So I changed the subject.

'Please look at the windows on the side. You can see people in wet suits diving in the pool from outside. It's pretty with the lights on.'

'A bit like a fish bowl.'

Again, I kept smiling. 'This pool is to make people

dream that they're deep in the ocean, not in the middle of the city.'

'And Japanese people love everything compact.'

'Exactly. And the convenience – you can learn to dive after work.'

He took several photos of the pool and I gave him the press release in English. He didn't need anything further for his article. I didn't need Naoki's help, but after Mr Lee left, I asked the assistant at the counter where Naoki was.

'He went on the early lunch shift,' she said with a pout.

Kyoko frowned when I told her about Naoki's early lunch.

'He promised me he'd be there. Maybe his boss changed his shift.'

I was pretty much convinced that Naoki was lying about his language skills. He must have run away instead of helping me as he did Kyoko. But I decided not to tell Kyoko yet. I needed some proof before disillusioning her.

The opportunity came earlier than I expected. The very next day, I returned from a meeting to find Naoki in our office for his tea break, chatting with Kyoko. He smiled, showing no guilt at seeing me.

'He's just got a certificate as a master of calligraphy,'

Kyoko said, before I opened my mouth. 'He's a collector of qualifications.'

In front of them was a weekly women's magazine, open at an article on self-improvement correspondence courses to boost your qualifications and earning power – the sort of article you often see in this kind of magazine. I was annoyed with Kyoko for being fooled so easily. Naoki looked at me straight in the eyes and for a moment he was challenging me. *Call me a liar, if you dare.*

'How wonderful,' I said, picking up the magazine. 'So, tell me which qualifications you have.' I read from the top of the list. 'Calligraphy?'

'The master certificate,' he said, with calm pride.

'Accounting?'

'I'm taking the first-grade course.'

'Boiler technician?'

'Ha ha, no.'

'Counselling children?'

'I've taken the basic course.'

You had to be very naïve to believe him, but he answered without hesitation. Kyoko didn't change her expression. I became irritated.

'Interior consultant?'

'Yes, I have the second grade.'

'Hang on,' I couldn't help interrupting. 'You have to be over twenty-five with interior designing experience to take the exam.'

Then he looked at me – not in his usual innocent way, but with cold anger.

'At my high school, there was a special course. Once we'd taken the class, we were qualified enough to be an interior coordinator. We just have to wait to twenty-five to be officially qualified.'

I knew enough about the qualification to be certain that what he was saying was complete bullshit. I had done several PR projects with interior designers. But there was something about him that meant I couldn't say it straight out. He scared me now. It was not the lying itself so much as his cold eyes . . . I realized that I had pushed him too far. I had cornered him in a cul-de-sac and he was forced to reveal himself . . .

I shot a glance at Kyoko. She, too, was astonished to see the anger in her favourite boy. But she knew what she had to do. She took the magazine from my hand.

'Graphic design?' she continued, going down the list.

'I . . . I learned it at school.'

'Proofreading?'

'I'm qualified for the second level.'

'Music editing?'

'I have a friend working at a sound studio and he taught me the basics.'

As Kyoko went down the list, I could see that Naoki was regaining his energy. His smile returned. He began to answer as convincingly as ever and became a nice boy again – even if we all knew he was lying. I admired the way Kyoko remained calm and even smiled at him occasionally. That was probably the secret of how she had become the company's top sales person. There were about twenty titles on the list, and he was apparently qualified for all but two of them. I couldn't bear to listen by the end because it was getting too painful, so I welcomed an incoming phone call and grabbed the receiver. Kyoko managed to reach to the bottom of the list and gave Naoki a 'Well done!' smile. Then she, too, had to answer a call and Naoki left the room.

When we had both finished our phone calls, silence fell in the office. Then Kyoko turned to the window.

'You know what?' she said. 'Before you came back, we were talking about those flowers . . .'

She pointed at the pots of Saintpaulia by the window.

'I told him how small they were when a stylist gave them to me and how I had managed to nurture them . . . Then he said he has the same flowers at home and he has managed to mix different types. Now he has white flowers with purple dots . . .' She sighed. 'Purple dots, you know?'

For a couple of days, there were no inquiries about the diving section, so I didn't have to face Naoki. He didn't come up to our office, although I knew Kyoko occasionally went there to say hi to the staff, including Naoki. She had a big heart. Maybe she had even known about Naoki from the start.

For my part, I was somewhat ashamed of myself and tried to avoid Naoki. I wondered why I had had to push him that far – after all, he was just a trainee.

'It's probably because you can speak languages,' Kyoko would say. 'Because you've lived abroad yourself. You are living in Naoki's fantasy life. And it's all reality to you.'

I didn't know what other people thought about Naoki's stories. Few would be as sympathetic as Kyoko. All I knew was that the rumours about him, such as studying at the University of Beijing, being the son of a shareholder, had died down. People no longer talked about Naoki.

Soon I was told by the main PR office to reduce media coverage of the diving pool. It was a strategic decision, partly because we had already had a lot of publicity and didn't want to risk over-exposure. But also, I saw the sales figures for the diving pool, which were not good. It had been expensive to build in the first place, but it was too small to hold proper lessons for advanced divers, so the pool's use was limited to absolute beginners and equipment tests. This wasn't enough to make a profit. Some staff complained that it had been insane to go ahead with the idea of a diving pool in the first place. It was more a PR stunt than a business proposition, they said. They even discussed the possibility of selling the facility to sports clubs.

On the way home that night, I passed the diving pool. *The pool is to make people dream that they are deep in the ocean, not in the middle of the city.* How many times had I said that to journalists? It was already dark and the light was off, so I couldn't see anything. If you didn't know, you wouldn't think there was a massive water tank in front of you.

Even if the pool wasn't making a profit, I would tell journalists it was doing very well. I had explained so much about diving, although I'd never tried it myself. Then I remembered what I had told Naoki: *But I feel like I have, after talking about our diving pool so much to journalists.*

He must have thought that PR was his ideal job.

Shortly afterwards, however, I discovered that Naoki had gone further.

It was the day I delivered photocopies of the pages of magazines in which their product was featured to the diving section. This was part of our routine, to keep the sales staff updated about what was in the media in case a customer asked about it. Mr Tanabe, the manager of the diving section, flipped through the pages and spotted a mistake.

'They say the new wet suits come in five different colours.' He pointed to the sentence. 'But we only have black.'

I called the magazine's editor, who was surprised to hear what I said.

'I called you before we went to press to confirm the details,' she said. 'I'm sure this is what you told me.'

'Did *I* tell you that?'

'Hang on, I'll get my proof copy . . . No, I don't think you were there, but your colleague answered. Is Mr Yamada working with you?'

'Yamada?'

'Yes, I remember. A very friendly young man answered my call and he was very helpful . . .'

I reported this to Mr Tanabe.

'It was Naoki, wasn't it?' He sighed.

'He must have been in our office while both Kyoko and I were out,' I said. 'It could have been during his tea break.'

'Sorry about the trouble he caused. He meant to be helpful, I'm sure.'

'I know . . . But . . .'

'I'll tell him that he can't do things beyond his role. I'll tell him there are boundaries.'

Now I wondered if Naoki understood the boundary between fantasy and reality. The boundary between the harmless lie and a deception that broke the rules of honest business . . .

'I'll leave it to you,' I said to Mr Tanabe. 'But I've learned that Naoki is . . .'

'He didn't go to the University of Beijing, if that's what you mean.'

'No, I didn't believe that from the start.'

'He's just an ordinary guy from a small high school, with average grades, from an average family. He didn't lie on his CV to get a job or anything. He just likes . . . to make himself look larger than life. We don't know why . . . But this is a different story, to make things up to journalists or customers.'

When I told Kyoko about this she looked distressed, feeling somehow responsible.

'I shouldn't have encouraged him so much, raving on about how helpful he was for PR . . .'

'It's not your fault. It's nobody's fault. Maybe not even his . . . He just can't help himself.'

'No one believes him now in the diving section.' She sighed. 'He's pretty isolated. He knows he lost us as well . . . He's realized that he's lost his whole audience.'

'So maybe he's trying to reach out further for someone who'll believe his stories . . .'

Soon I heard that Naoki was moved from the diving section to work at the counter selling sports towels –

where less consultation with customers was required.

Kyoko told me that her back was getting better, and she wanted to return to sales, so long as she didn't have to stand all day. She missed dealing directly with customers and the feeling of achievement in meeting sales targets. She missed the sense of reality. As for me, PR was the only thing I had ever done, or wanted to do, in the department store. I was offered a pay rise and was told to plan a campaign to sustain the current media attention into the next year. But I knew that media coverage would be quieter once we lost the sparkle of being a new store. Secret plans were under discussion to sell the diving pool. We also knew the Japanese economy was slowing down and we wouldn't sustain the gross sales of the last year. Reality would creep in. Still, I announced publicly that we were expecting a sales boost at Christmas.

Perhaps people would stop believing me.

Several weeks later, someone called me: 'Ms Kawano!'

I turned around and it was Naoki, smiling innocently as always. I hadn't seen him for a while and he had had his hair cut shorter.

'Great to see you on the sports floor.' He smiled in a friendly manner. 'A TV shoot today?'

'No. I've come down on my tea break . . .'

'Oh, for shopping?'

'No.' I hesitated. 'I've just registered for diving lessons next month.'

'Wow, are you finally going to go diving?'

'Why not, while I can do it with the staff discount?'

Or while the pool was still there . . . Or to think about how to make it work . . . But I couldn't tell him that.

'How about you?' I said. 'Have you tried the pool?'

'No, actually,' he said. 'And it's a bit too late.'

'Why?'

'I was going to tell you that . . . this is my last day.'

'Oh? I didn't know that . . . Does Kyoko know?'

'No. I was going to go up to your office to tell both of you. Thank you for everything, and it was a great pleasure working with you.'

'Thank you for your help . . .' I said, and I couldn't help asking, 'What are you going to do next?'

'My family is moving to Australia. My father's starting a business there and I'm going to help him.'

I looked at him and he looked straight back at me. He smiled, and I couldn't help liking his smile. Yet my heart sank a little. I hoped there was some truth in what he said, even just a word. We all wanted to believe in the fantasy.

'Good luck with whatever you do in the future,' I said.

'Thanks.' And he smiled, just like an innocent child.

What's in a Name?

Kachi A. Ozumba

A baby boy. A baby boy at last. At long last.

Seated on my bed in the sparsely furnished hospital room, I gazed on my baby with such intense emotion, such intense love. My womb still ached from the labour of the previous day. But it was the sweet dull ache of relief, of accomplishment. I have not disappointed my husband. All those years that he stood by me, resisting the pressure to take a second wife or to send me packing. I closed my eyes in a heartfelt prayer of thanks.

For more than six years I had laboured to bear a son. Ozoemena, my husband, having lost his brothers to the Biafran war, was the only surviving son of his parents. He was therefore seen as bearing the responsibility for the continuation of his lineage. My mother-in-law had impressed this well on me before our marriage.

The door to my room swung open after a gentle knock. My husband and our four daughters bustled in. The youngest was almost three years old, while the oldest was six and a half. They were accompanied by their favourite uncle, Okwudili.

'Mummy, good morning,' they chorused, rushing towards my bed.

'Mummy, where's baby? Daddy said you have brought him out from your tummy,' said the youngest, as I caressed her fat cheeks. She quickly noticed that her sisters had crowded round an object in the room and rushed to join them. 'Let me see, *let me seeee . . .*' she cried, tugging at her sisters.

Her uncle had to lift her in his arms before she could see the baby lying quietly and staring with blank eyes in the old metal cot.

I gazed at my daughters and smiled languidly. Each of them represented a milestone in my long search for a male child. And each of their native names told a story. Six months into our marriage we had been blessed with a baby girl. My husband, since he returned from his prolonged period of study in Britain, had built for himself a reputation as a deviant where native customs were concerned. So no one had raised an eyebrow when, instead of taking his first child to his parents for christening, he had insisted we christened her ourselves. Furthermore, being a believer in gender equality, he had stated that I had even more right than he did to name our child, since I was the one that bore her in my womb and delivered her. Nevertheless I asked him to name our first child. He called her Margaret.

'A beautiful name for a beautiful girl,' he had said, smiling.

I do not like Western names. I feel they are largely arbitrary and meaningless. My in-laws had been rather disappointed that our first child turned out to be a girl. So, as a second name, I called her Nwanyibuife, which means 'A girl is something of worth'.

Two years later, I gave birth to another girl. It was then that the pressures from my in-laws really began. My husband tried to placate them, telling them about the X and Y chromosomes, and explaining that the man played a vital role in determining the sex of a child. But they said he had allowed himself to be brainwashed by the white man's sophistry, and cursed the day he left for the white man's land to read away his common sense. They insinuated that my womb was filled with girls alone. It was painful. I had answered them by christening the girl Chinenyenwa, which means 'It is the Lord who gives children'.

Chinenyenwa was soon weaned and I became pregnant again. When my mother-in-law learned about my condition, she sent Aunty Eliza, her husband's cousin, to me on a special mission. Aunty Eliza was a retired nurse; good-natured, she was the kind of person who got along with everyone. We were quite close, and it was often said in our extended family that she was the only one to whom I listened.

She had knocked on our door one foggy morning, clutching a market bag. My husband had already left for work, so I was alone in the house with Margaret and Chinenyenwa, who had just started to crawl. We sat in the parlour, chatting, while she kept reaching into the bag, retrieving different native condiments and delicacies, some of which were deemed especially good for pregnant women. The smells soon mixed and swirled around in the room, reminding me of my mother-in-law's kitchen in the village.

The last item Aunty Eliza produced from the bag was a green schnapps bottle. The bottle was corked with dried grass.

'You know what this is?' she had asked, holding the bottle up for my inspection.

'Is it not palm oil?' I said.

The contents of the bottle were just as dark and thick as palm oil. Moreover, such green schnapps bottles were the favourite choice of palm oil sellers for bottling their product.

She shook her head. 'This is a medicine from Ezen-wanyi Dibia. I'm sure you have heard of her, the greatest midwife and herbalist in the whole of Igboland.'

I nodded.

'You should take it every day – two spoonfuls in the morning and two at night – and you can be sure that the baby forming in your womb will be male.

Like you, my friend Mama Ejima had problems having a male child, but after taking this medicine she delivered twins, both male, and her husband slaughtered a goat in her honour.'

'Thank you, Aunty,' I had said, as she handed me the bottle. I did not know what else to say, I felt so confused. I pulled out the grass cork, took a whiff of the contents and was thrown into a fit of sneezing.

'You see how strong it is?'

I nodded, wiping the tears from my eyes and sneezing some more.

'Yes, we women have our ways too,' she continued. 'In some matters we should trust our mothers and do things the way they did. Let me tell you something, my daughter. Your husband is a man, a very good man. But like every other man, deep down in his heart, he wants a son. He may smile, laugh and talk now as if he does not mind having only girls. But believe me, my daughter, he won't be able to hold his smile on for much longer if you continue to give him only girls. Don't fail to take this medicine. He doesn't have to know about it.'

That night when I told my husband what had transpired between his aunt and myself, he laughed heartily. His laughter was infectious and soon I was laughing with him. But my gaze never left his mouth.

'If my mother asks, tell her you drank it all to the last drop, to the *very* last drop,' he had said, holding the green bottle, inverted, over the toilet to ensure no drop was left in it.

A few months later I gave birth to a baby girl. I could not help wondering if Ezenwanyi's medicine would have made any difference. I pushed the thought out of my mind and called our new daughter Chimamanda, 'My Lord will not fail (me)'. My husband had taken one look at her ebony colour – our other children had taken after my lighter skin – and said, 'This one is Junior, Ozoemena Junior. Who says a girl can't bear her father's name, especially when it's a unisex name?'

That became her first name. Although I was happy with my husband's wholehearted acceptance of our new baby girl, a cynical part of my mind hoped he was not sending me a subtle message, for the name Ozoemena means 'May it not happen again'.

That night, I had a dream in which I saw my parents-in-law standing in a field littered with guns and corpses. They were both staring lovingly at the baby boy cradled in my mother-in-law's arms. Their gaze moved from the baby to the corpses before them, then swung up to the skies as they called out with earnest, begging voices, 'Ozoemena.'

Then they disappeared and my husband materialized. He was holding our new daughter in the crook of his left arm and wagging the index finger of his right hand at me: 'Ozoemena.'

When it was morning, I told my husband about my dream. He shook his head sadly. 'Don't allow yourself to become paranoid about this whole thing,' he had said, and smiled to reassure me.

I just kept staring at his lips.

When I conceived for the fourth time, my mother-in-law had left the village to take up residence with us in the city. As she watched my stomach swelling, she found subtle ways to remind me of my obligation to produce an heir for her son. She would launch into disturbing tales of what happened in cases where one woman or the other proved incapable of doing just that.

'Eziokwu,' she would usually begin, affirming the veracity of the tale she was about to relate, 'our neighbour in the village, Papa Obi, accompanied by other elders in his clan, took a stout-hipped maiden to his son in the city. They sat him and his wife down and said, "Our son, this is your second wife. Her name is Nkobuna. We have fulfilled all the customs and married her for you. All you have to do is show her you are your father's son. Your father fathered seven strong sons, and the offspring of a lion cannot be a grass-eater."'

After each tale, she would laugh with a toothy grin and clap her hands thrice, like bantering market women. Then, still showing me her teeth, she would launch into another tale, pushing her message down my throat the way I pushed bitter pills, buried in balls of garri, down Margaret's throat whenever she had malaria.

An agonizing disappointment was born with the birth of our fourth girl. My husband called her Barbara, and her first name was my cry born of desperation to the Lord: 'Chitiogwa, "The Lord grant us variety".'

It must have been in answer to that cry that we were granted this – our baby boy.

'Mummy, what's baby's name?' Margaret suddenly asked, staring at me with my eyes.

'Mummy, let his name be Rotimi, eh?' Chinenyenwa suggested. 'My friend in school, his name is Rotimi.'

'No. If you call him Rotimi he will have big teeth like Uncle Rotimi, my music teacher,' Margaret said, and pushed out her upper teeth like a squirrel.

'But my friend Rotimi does not have big teeth.'

'That's because he's still small. When he grows big like Uncle Rotimi he will have big teeth.'

They chattered on, arguing over the baby's name. Junior watched them quietly, thumb in mouth, while Chitiogwa still nestled in her uncle's arms. Soon their uncle took them out to buy them ice cream.

My husband came to my bedside. He stooped and planted a breezy kiss on my cheek. I felt the reassuring tickle of his moustache and the metallic touch of his spectacles. He straightened up and turned towards the baby.

'Darling, I hope I didn't take too long?' he asked, bending over the cot. 'And how are you this morning?'

Ever since he had set eyes on our new baby, he had been acting like an infatuated teenager. He had insisted on spending the night in the hospital in order to attend to the baby whenever he awoke at night while I was resting. He had even missed his favourite sitcom, *Happy Times*, although there was a television in the room. He would sit for long spells of time gazing at the baby, then, occasionally, his hand would reach out to touch him – as if to reassure himself that this was no mirage. It was a very reluctant father who left the hospital in the morning to go and fetch our daughters.

I studied my husband. He was staring at the baby with that dreamy look in his eyes again. I wondered if at that moment I still existed in his consciousness. I decided to intrude upon his thoughts.

'Hmm, I'm sure you would not have been acting this way if it had been another girl,' I teased.

'But, darling,' he protested, turning to face me with an aggrieved expression, 'I've told you time and again that I don't really mind the sex of our children. Even if it had been another girl I would still have been as happy. A home of girls can be fun . . . and profitable too,' he added, trying to make a joke. 'You know, Mr Nwakaego is planning to replace his rickety Peugeot 504 car with all the money he'll collect as bride price on the heads of his six daughters.'

I smiled. 'But you never did a third of all you're doing now when our daughters were born. Do you remember that when Chitiogwa was born you left me with the baby all night in the hospital, saying you had to look after our girls at home?'

'But then there was no uncle around to stand in for me at home. Look, darling, let's not waste words on such matters, let's talk of more important things . . . like the name of our son.'

He stared at me as if expecting a response. I said nothing, so he continued. 'I have the perfect first name for him,' he said, beaming at me. 'A name made in heaven for him.'

'What's the name?' I asked.

'Churchill,' he said. 'Churrrr-chillll,' he repeated slowly, as if savouring the taste of the name on his lips.

'I don't like the name. It just doesn't sound well in my ears and doesn't sit well in my heart. Besides, why should our first son bear an English name as his first name? How many English children bear Igbo names?' I queried.

'Darling, you should not be so racist about these things. The world is becoming a global village and racial barriers are fast thinning out. I have always admired Winston Churchill and would like our son to be inspired by his greatness,' he explained.

'I really don't like the name for a first name,' I repeated, shaking my head.

My husband became silent. I could see I had hurt his feelings. His voice was quite cool when he asked, 'All right, what name do you suggest?'

'Darling, can't we call him Adimungupu?' I asked, trying to sound conciliatory. The name means 'I am not excluded (from the ranks of male-children bearers)'.

'Oh, so the child's name should just reflect your new status, eh? Don't you think . . .'

My husband went no further. The door burst open. My mother-in-law, buxom and fat, waddled in. Her feet, in their rubber slippers, were still brown with village dust. The old blue ogodo of their local church's women's guild which she had on oozed the stale sweaty smell of a long journey. Behind her, leaning on a cane, was my father-in-law. He was tall, wizened and thin – a much older version of my husband. For a man who had retired from the civil service twelve years previously, he was still very strong. Apparently they had set out on the journey upon receiving the news, which my husband had sent them just the evening before.

'Ah! Papa, Mama, what a pleasant surprise,' my

husband exclaimed. 'You got here so fast. You must have taken a jet from the village.'

My husband hugged his parents. I pushed myself up from the bed and joined in the greetings. My in-laws were brusque in their response. It seemed they could not wait to brush us aside and head straight for the cot.

'Ewooooo! Ozo-nwam,' cried my mother-in-law, calling her son by his pet name and lifting the baby in her arms. 'This is you all over again. My daughter, you have done well,' she added, casting a glance my way.

My father-in-law ran his tongue over his lips. It was a slow movement and seemed more like that of a man licking palm wine from his lips than that of one moistening harmattan-cracked lips. He took the baby from his wife.

'At last,' he muttered. 'At long last.' He held the baby up and stared long at him, the way he must have stared at my husband when he was born, after the demise of his brothers. His eyes brimmed with tears. He turned to his wife and said in a quivering voice, 'Now I can sing like Simeon: "Lord, now lettest thou thy servant depart in peace . . ."' He broke into a rusty version of the Nunc Dimittis, flashing a set of teeth still kept in good condition by his son's regular care.

He stopped as suddenly as he started, handed the baby to his wife and reached for the raffia bag still hanging from his left shoulder. He retrieved a small bottle of kai-kai, the exceedingly strong, locally brewed gin used in traditional ceremonies. He unscrewed the cap on the bottle. The heady smell began to spread faintly through the room.

Holding the opened bottle in one hand, he poured a libation of thanks to his ancestors, praying his joy into every drop that he spilled for them on the hard terrazzo of the hospital floor. He then wet his fingers with the gin, placed them gently on the baby's head and pronounced, 'Afamefuna Amamechina, welcome.'

Afamefuna means 'May my name not be lost', while Amamechina means 'May my lineage not come to an end'.

The pronouncement jolted my husband back to life from the spell of watching what looked like the carefully plotted script of his parents. He was quickly beside his father, protesting, 'But, Dad, we already have names . . .'

'Shut your mouth,' his father cut in angrily. 'You think this is going to be like the other cases, in which you named my grandchildren without even consulting me? I just did not bother because, after all, they are girls who will soon grow up, marry and bear their husbands' names. Now, if you think I would also fold my arms and watch you do the same with my first grandson, then you are greatly mistaken. I have pronounced his names. It is sealed with God and our ancestors. You know better than to refuse to accept them. The son who tries to wrestle with his father gets blinded by his father's loincloth!'

My husband shook his head at his father. But I could see in his eyes that he was struggling with his doubts.

His father stormed out of the room.

My mother-in-law handed the baby to me and ran after her husband, slamming the door in her haste. The baby, startled by the sound, stirred and blinked. Then his tiny eyes squeezed shut as his cry pierced the silence of the room like an alarm bell.

'Afamefuna Amamechina, keep quiet,' my husband muttered, and puckered his lips.

The Last Mouthful

Saman Shad

'Open your eyes, Mina.'

Her eyes slowly willed themselves to part. Bright sunlight flooded in, each beam shining with the vigour of a new day. Blinding her temporarily. Leading her to see only shadows and red, blue flashes.

'Mina.' The voice asserted itself again. 'Mina.'

Who is it? This person? Is it a person?

The dark shape of their oval head appears before her, shadowed by the light. Ammy, she swiftly thinks. Warm rays of comfort pulsate through her. Suddenly the load of that heavy metal plate, that grey, antiseptic metal that clanged inside of her, that acted like a hollow dead weight impeding her every breath, is lifted. Suddenly, everything is better. Her heart feels lighter. As if it is able to beat with a normal rhythm again. A rhythm that reminded her of the dhol they played at weddings. Doof-doof! Doof-doof! Each slap of the drum driving the beat forward.

'Ammy!' she almost squealed with excitement. With relief.

'No, no, Mina. Not Ammy. Aunty,' the shadowy voice says slowly. 'Aunty.' The repetition of the word hammers that rusty nail even deeper through her heart.

But she is unwilling to give up. She wants to hold on to it, that brief little speck of a moment, when suddenly life seemed to shine again. When for a minuscule instant she had recaptured hope.

'Ammy?'

'No, Mina, no,' her aunt repeats patiently. 'Ammy is dead.'

Three round, milky-brown biscuits sit on a little white plate. To her they look like a face. The face of a ghost wailing. Its two blank eyes dead. Its mouth forever frozen in a howl. A howl that perhaps never had time to escape.

Her aunt sighs. Her first day here and already she was a Burden. A Picky Eater. A Problem Child. She'd been presented with a variety of foods, the names of many of which she hadn't heard before, and refused them all.

Tuna sandwiches, they'd called them. But they smelt like something the cats in her alley ate from the gutter. Nutella on toast, they said. But it was brown and sticky and didn't look too appetizing. Jaffa cakes – 'Look, it's chocolate. Choc-o-late,' they repeated slowly. Trying to entice her in some way. Not mentioning the orange goo oozing out from the middle.

She didn't want to say she never really ate chocolate. That she'd never liked the taste of it when, on occasion, she'd had some. When her second and third cousins back home had saved their rupees and bought the expensive treat and hid themselves behind the cupboard in the living room, away from all the little nuisances like herself, and gorged themselves before they were finally found out. Back then she had pretended to be curious about it. Pretended to want it so bad that she cried and nagged them into giving her a bite. She'd tried hard to hide the look of distaste that unfolded across her face as soon as she'd popped the brown block in her mouth and felt it melting on her tongue, the horrible bittersweet aftertaste quickly moving to the corners of her mouth.

'Get the digestives,' her aunt had said to her cousins as a last resort. They didn't hear her, occupied as they were by a toothy man in a bright, patterned jacket on TV. 'Digestives! Digestives!' her aunt exclaimed, as one of them slowly dragged himself off to do as she asked.

Her aunt didn't look like she moved much. She had big meaty upper arms that reminded Mina of chicken thighs attached to narrow little chicken legs – those being her aunt's lower arms. Her body seemed to be squeezing itself out of her shirt, the flesh creating a river of ripples down her sides, straining to be let loose from its confines. Her aunt's body didn't seem to belong to her head, which was small and oval, like her Ammy's. Oh, no. No, no, she must not do that. She must not remind herself of that. She must stop that. Stop that! Stop it! But it was too late.

'She's crying again, Muuuum,' her cousin who came bearing the face of a ghost on a plate casually stated to his mother, who too had become distracted by the excitable loud man on TV.

'Hain? What? Oh, no, Mina. You must not. You have cried enough. You mustn't cry any more.'

Mina pretended to understand. Knew it was for the best. She gritted her teeth and gave a firm nod. But the tears didn't stop. They kept flowing and flowing, as they had done from the moment her world had come to an end.

Her aunt tsked and dabbed Mina's face with a worn kitchen towel that had once been used to wipe spills and surfaces. Its rough texture scraped her tears and scratched her nose. She had been crying so much, they had stopped wasting tissues on her. 'Chi, chi, so many tissues. They don't come for free, you know,' her aunt had said. Already she was starting to become aware of her status as a Financial Burden. At least she wasn't just a single type of Burden.

'Look,' her aunt said. 'They are only biscuits. Only plain, simple biscuits. Eat them. You must. Eat them.'

Her aunt seemed to like repeating herself. Perhaps she had learned that repetition created conviction.

And when you spoke with conviction, people obeyed your every word.

'Eat!' she said. 'Eat! Eat!' Her face didn't display any emotion. She didn't seem upset or angry. She was just compelled to ensure that Mina ate. It was of the utmost importance that some form of food went into Mina's mouth.

Mina didn't want to prove her aunt's repetition theory wrong, so she picked up one of the ghost's eyes (better to have one eye and one mouth, Mina thought, than two eyes and no mouth) and bit into it. Her aunt smiled with satisfaction. The bone-dry biscuit broke into tiny crumbs on Mina's tongue and went straight down her thirsty throat, causing her to choke.

'Arre, what's wrong with you, you silly girl? Didn't they feed you biscuits back in Pakistan?'

Mina knew her aunt didn't mean to be so insensitive. Perhaps she thought that since Mina didn't speak much, she didn't understand the words being spoken to her, so it didn't really matter what was said in front of her. Or so Mina liked to think.

Her aunt's first few calls for water went unheard, but finally they got through and one of the sisters went to answer it.

When Mina had drunk a full glass of water and her tears and coughs had died down, her aunt asked again what it was she wanted to eat. But Mina didn't know how to tell her. In a place where they just ate dry foods like bread and biscuits all day, how could they understand?

'Maybe you should sleep and we will start fresh tomorrow. Hain?'

Sleep seemed to be the agreed form of escape for both Mina and her aunt. Though it was still daylight outside, it was as if they both preferred this option. Even at this age, Mina knew that, being young, she could will her body into sleep no matter what the time or situation. She looked at the adults around her, who had no choice but to be bogged down by the awful reality of the world, and she knew she was lucky to be able to dream when she wanted.

Upstairs in bed, Mina ignored the beams of sunlight that wanted to barge through the curtains and excitedly tell her, *Look, it's sunny outside. It's time to play. Come out and play, Mina! There's still time for fun.*

She resolutely shut her eyes against them. She was not going to be distracted by their superficial folly. They were not going to take her away from the far better world of dreams that awaited her. Sure, lately the dreams hadn't been so good. But she remembered her grandmother telling her that no dreams were bad. You should never say dreams are bad, dreams are just dreams. And they are always good. If you have a nightmare, just take it as a sign. But never say it was bad.

She wished she had asked her grandmother why that was so. Why you should never say you'd had a bad dream. But she hadn't. And now of course it was too late.

She remembered her grandmother covering her face with her white dupatta and turning away from her as she left for the airport, as if the sight of Mina reminded her of a thought more painful than she could bear.

Mina – the tiny splinter of pain everyone desperately wanted to remove.

She closed her eyes and willed the dreams to take her. Whether they were good or not so good, they were still taking her away from here. And anything had to be better than here.

Her three English cousins, two girls and one boy, who were between three and eight years older than her, didn't seem too taken by her. Initially she'd been a momentary distraction. They'd pinched her cheeks and smiled at her charitably. But soon the call from the glowing box in the corner of their living room became too hard for any of them to ignore. So they spent most of their time kneeling in front of it with mouths wide open, like worshippers at a temple.

Back home, Mina remembered, they didn't really watch TV. There never seemed any time for it. Days were full of school and of playing with cousins, and neighbours, and friends of friends of friends, and of eating food from street carts despite the many adult warnings against it, and sure, of getting the occasional beating, which did sting initially but they were just slaps and no one really took such things to heart, and of filling your lungs with the brown Karachi air as you ran down muddy alleyways, and of washing yourself with warm water from buckets and cold water from taps, and of being fed by hand morsels of food which at the time didn't taste like anything spectacular, but which now seemed to be the tastiest meals ever cooked.

Mina's stomach rumbled at the thought.

Sometimes, when there were many of them, because most of the time the house seemed to be overrun by a whole host of people, all the kids would gather and sit in a circle around her grandmother, who sat bearing a large plate of food. One by one, into each of their mouths, she would pop fingerfuls of food which they would then quickly devour. But no matter how hungry you were, you had to wait your turn. Mina remembered her mouth salivating when she knew she was just one child away, and also the fights some of them would get in about who'd had the bigger mouthful.

But it was the last mouthful everyone wanted. No matter whose turn it was, the last mouthful was a free for all. Because the one who ate the last mouthful was lucky. 'If you eat the last mouthful of food,' she remembers being told, 'then you will get the same amount of strength as if you had eaten all the food on the plate yourself. And that means you are very fortunate.'

Usually the last mouthful went to the youngest or best-behaved child, which mostly meant that Mina got to eat it.

But none of that mattered now, of course. Here you could eat a whole plateful, or could, in the case of her English cousins, pick at half the plate of food and throw the other half in the bin. The sight of which had made her wince. There were no lucky mouthfuls of food here. Or perhaps the lucky mouthfuls were the ones that actually got eaten.

Mina squeezed her eyes shut. Come on, sleep. This should be easy. It always had been. But her stomach continued to grumble. Why hadn't she eaten all that strange food they'd offered her? On the few occasions she had complained about what she was eating back home, she had just been told she was lucky to be able to eat. Lucky to have a meal in front of her. And hungry people ate whatever was given to them. So if she wasn't so hungry, perhaps she should come back when she was. That was usually enough to stop any complaints.

Not counting, of course, that period around three years ago when she went through her 'choosy' phase.

Lying here, starving, reminded her of what it was like then. She was five years old and refused to eat food from anyone but her mother. Except her mother was much too busy to feed her three times a day.

Everyone would complain, 'Arre, Rukhsana, your daughter is becoming a nuisance. She won't eat from us. It's because you make her think she's a princess. Tell her she's nothing of the sort. Give her a slap on the head and knock such ideas out of her.'

But, of course, her mother paid no attention to them.

Her Ammy was perennially busy in the kitchen. She seemed on a constant mission of cooking, feeding and washing up after her in-laws. Sometimes Mina would come and watch her, surrounded by huge blackened pots sitting on open flames with various curries bubbling inside, a stack of dirty silver plates on the floor, and hot chapattis browning on an over-turned pan. As the only daughter-in-law in the house, her mother was responsible for everything that came in and out of the kitchen. If her in-laws weren't satisfied, she wasn't doing her job.

During that short-lived period, Mina ate only once or twice a day, determined as she was to be fed by her mother. Though it meant she would sometimes wake up in the middle of the night, ravenous. Her mother, who lay beside her, thoroughly exhausted and softly snoring, somehow always knew her daughter had woken. They would both then quietly get up and creep into the kitchen.

Mina could still feel the coolness of the tiles under her feet as she tiptoed down the corridor. Her mother would walk silently ahead of her, sometimes putting her hand out in the darkness of the night to reach for Mina, to help guide her or perhaps hurry her along.

In the kitchen her mother would light a candle and, under its flickering glow, put two slices of white bread that was meant for next morning's breakfast on a plate and heat some milk on the stove. She would then sit Mina on the tiny kitchen windowsill and feed her sweet pieces of bread dipped in warm milk. The night breeze blowing over from the docks of Karachi would gently fan them as Mina and her mother whispered to each other, their voices drifting like sighs in the middle of the night.

Mina could picture her Ammy's eyes as they were then. Tired, with dark circles and a weariness that made her seem older than she was. But there was something else, a tiny little glimmer that sparkled beneath it all. Mina knew that her mother didn't mind waking up to feed her. Perhaps, maybe, she cherished it as much as Mina did.

Thinking of her Ammy feeding her then somehow made Mina feel better now. She didn't even want to cry. And it was OK anyway, because she could feel the tug of the dream world pulling her closer. Closer, closer, till she couldn't see anything but the warm darkness of the sky back home, just before it rained.

The air was thick and heavy with humidity. As if a blanket had been drawn over all of them. But no one seemed to mind, because the rain washed away the dirt from the streets and gave everyone a moment of respite from the relentless heat.

But, best of all, when it rained, everyone you knew would run out and get drenched. Completely and absolutely drenched. And everywhere you looked you saw all those you loved with their hands in the air, getting thoroughly wet, wearing big, untainted smiles on their faces, calling for you to join them.

Care and Control

Neil Wellappili

The sunrays beam through the barred windows and I know I'm fucked. Fucked like the urban legend of the mate of a mate of a mate of a mate who got put inside and then arse-scragged and decided he liked it and now scraghorns anyone you pay him to. That is an urban legend, right? Or maybe it's just my friends of friends of friends.

I'm trapped in the unit on a section 2. Sping. Marooned. Twenty-eight days of assessment because I lost my appeal. Sitting in the recreation room for the ward round, surrounded by eight pairs of goggling draconia eyes, I clam up. What the quantoes don't understand is maybe I stayed in my room the whole time because of the gangs outside my building that would kill me, interfere with me sexually, as soon as I stepped outside. Granted, there are Africans among the nursing staff, but as a black man in the system, I know the routine.

For a short period in my life, crack cocaine was a pain in my heart, a wheeze in my lungs and a suppurating pipe burn on my lips. But that was then. I don't need that stupidness for thirty pounds a pop. Dawn is beautiful. Parks are beautiful. Walking down Camden High Street is beautiful. I'm an outdoors man. I've ventured the entire tube map, foot soldier, bike, rollerskates. That's what I'm about. Explore. Learn.

So I sit in the caged recreation room, an electronic keyboard by the wall that only Greg the old punker plays, all of us perched on green plastic chairs with shiny black legs. The draconia consultant psychiatrist smiles at me, nefarious.

'Carl, it seems that you're still suspicious. Could you tell us a bit more about that?'

Too fucking right I'm suspicious. I'm dragged here on the whim of a community mental health team that has consistently displayed a lack of regard for my person. He knows I know something's up. He knows I know he knows. I keep it together.

'How do you feel about the tribunal?' he asks, blatantly goading me.

A sharp intake of breath. 'The tribunal went against me this time. Prosecution you, defendant me, and I lost. Maybe it's for the best I stay here for a while. Everyone has problems.'

'But at the tribunal the consensus was your problems can only be dealt with here.'

'That's what I meant,' I say with a sigh. Of course, it's not what I mean at all; as far as I'm concerned, I'm not even ill. I could be doing so much more on the outside.

'Carl, take the incident with Richard, what happened then?'

'There was a bunch of us watching the rotnut and he comes in and pulls out the plug, so I thumped him.'

'How do you feel about that now?'

'I'll try to be nice to him. I wouldn't like to be him.'

He cut my leave, the vampireman. Cooped up on the unit, with only the concrete courtyard ten feet by ten feet to call outdoors. Our floor has maybe twenty patients, some of whom cocoon themselves in their rooms so you hardly ever see them. I walk the long pea-green corridor, lounge at one end, nurses' station at the other, door upon door either side: shared male bedrooms, dining room, kitchen, staff and patient bathrooms. I feel the strip lights flickering and it can give you migraines. The bars on the windows are not thick like in a jail, they're thin, more like a grille. The sole unbarred window is in the nurses' station, a square puddle of natural light in the halogen corridor.

Next to the nurses' station is a second corridor secured with an electronic key door, leading to the female bedrooms. If I approach the station from the side, I can hear them through the observation window, whispering about patients, sometimes about me. It's not like they're selestering against me, just saying something like, 'Carl needs to progress' or 'Carl needs to learn.'

There's piss on the corridor's mottled stone floor and the weary-looking Nigerian cleaner is tackling it. I smile at her as I pass. If ever there was a job I couldn't do. She doesn't smile back, probably thinks I did it. My money would be on Greta, middle-aged and evidently a long-term patient. She lurks near the nurses' station with big staring eyes, running her hands along the walls, repeating incoherent words in a childish high-pitched voice.

'Can I go to the shops now?' she'll ask a nurse when the time comes for her two hours of appointed leave. She will stare, perplexed, repeat the question every twenty seconds until the nurse comes over, hurriedly pulling on a coat and cooing with a kindly Tanzanian lilt. It hathes me that, since the Richard incident, Greta is allocated the same amount of leave as me.

I share a room with Terry Woods, our territories demarcated by a canvas divider. He knows where I'm coming from, he's had his run-ins too. He's in his mid-thirties, about ten years older than me, white, with prematurely grey stubble and a squint in his right eye that makes you think he's talking to someone behind your shoulder.

'He was a nice guy,' he says about Dennis Nilsen the first time we meet. 'Did time with him at Broadmoor. Very posh. Dennis the Menace. Knew this fella on the street he came on to. Guy in a suit told him to come round, have a shower and a meal. He'd put sleepers in your food and then strangle you. No pain at all, see. Except this fella had a tolerance for sleepers so he wakes up and goes, 'What the fuck?' and walks out sharpish, cos Dennis the Menace was only a little guy. This fella gets caught shoplifting a few days later and tells the police about him, but he's a homeless junkie and Nilsen's some ex-police stockbroker. So he has a few more people round before they catch him. He'd keep the bodies for a few days, play with them, whatever. Chop them up when they start to smell, put them in the freezer and flush them down the toilet. Told me there were three bodies no one knows about. He only got caught when the sewers blocked and the neighbours noticed the smell. Just a fella that felt for the homeless and enjoyed being naughty with dead bodies.' We laugh about that, Terry and me.

'It's like in Russia, there's a kid who says he's got X-ray vision. How do the Russians deal with it? They set him tests, put people with cancer in front of him and he can point it out. And I don't care what anyone says, that's God-given. Try any of that in England and you'd end up here. They tell you you're ill, slap a name on what you've got, and you've got to carry it around for life. If I hear voices, I talk back, simple as. It makes me feel silly but that's what calms me down. And unless you fight them,' he says, 'they dope you up on their nutpills and they're worse than the fucking illness.' Terry pauses, sated. It helps to have alliances in this place.

There was a suicide the week before I came. Girl in her twenties, he says, locked herself in the toilets and slit her wrists. Can still smell the blood when you go in. Thing is, he doesn't think she meant to die. He pulls back his sleeve and shows me the slashes on his left wrist. 'Cut crossways when you want attention. Normal person thinks, "Rah, that's mental!" but in prison, they know that's nothing. If you mean it, you cut longways, or at the elbow or at the neck. Not just a nick, you got to dig right into the artery and it comes out like this – tock tock tock.'

In the sitting room, they don't have table tennis or anything like that, there's just a rotnut, newspapers, paperbacks and some board games no one plays. Patients sit on the sofa, glued to the rotnut, always smoking, and I can feel it eating my lungs. It's the outer limits here, the benighted, the wild frontier. That thing with Richard happened when I was watching the news. I knew Anna Ford had something important to tell me because of the look on her face.

And in Tel Aviv, a suicide bomber blew himself up today, killing twelve bus passengers –

That's what made me snap, when he unplugged it, because I need to keep up with things.

I sit next to Rita the sex monster on the sofa. She

shuffled up to me in the corridor and gave me a hug, saying, 'You smell nice.' She stared at me with her washed-out blue eyes, flashing a skizzled grin. The rotnut vomits out an afternoon movie about some maniac on a plane. In the next seat is Barry Fishlips, discoursing on his favourite subject, Barry Fishlips. Corpulent white guy with chip-pan hair and tits, likes to talk about how many women he scraghorned on grotty Spanish holidays: 'And I took her out to the beach and she lifted up her skirt . . .' He never tires of regaling other mentally ill people with his un-doubtedly fictional sex adventures. I'd like to slap him about with a big stinking kipper, then point at it and say, 'This is you, this is you,' until I piss myself laughing.

'Where are you from?' Rita asks me. 'Your teeth are lovely and white.'

Rita the sex monster moves her hand further up my thigh and I squirm when she touches the tip of my krueger. I would run away screaming, but for the fact that the heating system blasts ions into the air that make me sluggish. I look across at her face and I can see blue veins under the parchment of her skin and the cigarette stains on her teeth. She's grinning at me again, ravenous. Richard, who is about sixty, sits in the corner, head buried in the paper.

'You like that, don't you?' Rita the sex zombie purrs. My eyes are bulging in terror and she interprets this as carnal delight. Rita the sex monster never blimmed at the quantoes and they loaded her on so much scroogies she walks like a robot, in tiny ballerina steps.

'You must get lonely in here, eh, Rita?' I manage, struggling against the ions to shift back a little in my seat.

'They're all really nice in here,' she lisps, 'very accommodating.'

'Rita, when will you get better, get outside?' I yammer.

'When I'm ready. They say I'm getting better.'

'How long have they kept you in here?'

'Now why would you want to know that?'

Some people are cagey about broaching intimacies such as their length of stay. I'm struggling to break free. Omar would not approve and I'm glad he is not witness to my predicament. 'In Algeria, there was a cruel cruel war,' he told me. 'I come to this country. God created the buildings outside, God created the animals, God created the plants, God created the seas . . .' They loaded Omar on the scroogies too. His muscles constantly selester against him, head jerking from side to side, mandible jutting, grimacing and grunting to an off-kilter rhythm. He walks with each leg bent at the knee, tottering haphazardly, leaning against the wall. 'God gave me a beautiful face. I was devil. I used to do devil things. I knew Turkish girls,

Indian girls, Jamaican girls, everyone loved me. I love people to love me. Illegal sex is haram. Shayatin will cause you to have illegal sexual relations.'

Something in Rita's features suggests she was much prettier before the quantoes interfered. She sweets me up because I'm the only one she hasn't joobered yet. Me, I was never a connoisseur of the drug-related jangalang, the quickly forgotten scraghorn, type you get in Streatham dispensing twenty-five-pound suck-jobs, so I overpower the ions and escape.

'The only way to beat an alligator is to gouge its eyes out. Grab it round the back and thumb one of its eyes, then it'll run away. Try hitting it on the head with a hammer and it'll fucking laugh at you,' Terry says.

Nature's one of the main things we talk about when we're in the room together. What the subjis outside don't understand is that something is afoot on the unit. Me and Terry understand, it's a feeling we get being here, and it's not easy to explain. Terry says he's been feeling this since before the girl died in the toilet, like the clouds are gathering, a bad feeling in the air.

'Antarctica. To me, that's no man's land,' he says.

'If this were Antarctica, you'd be Scott and I'd be Oates,' I tell him, 'fearless adventurers.'

'Scott of the Antarctic? He killed himself, didn't he? You're a comfort, you are, you're a gem.'

When I tell him about Rita, he's not surprised. There's a patient he likes, Sylvia. She's Swedish and prefers being called Mathilda. He says she's with one of the male nightshift nurses, he hears them at it in her room. She walks past when we step out of our room, her ample firm behind encased in a flesh-coloured miniskirt.

'Hello, boys,' she says, her voice high-pitched and monotonous. Terry grins back at her, then mimes grabbing her buttocks once she passes, legs jigging on the stone floor in glee.

'Richard, we need to ask you some questions,' Terry says as we sit down with him. He wears a white dressing gown with a thicket of bands wrapped around each wrist and several strings around his neck, including one bearing an icon of the Virgin Mary. A white beard stretches from his sideburns to his chin and his gaunt face is topped by shoulder-length white hair. He sits his bony arse on Terry's bed and stares us down.

'Abandon hope all ye who enter here.' They should have that written above the door. When we're in the black, there's no coming back. Barry's a dangerous psychopath, Barry Barber he calls himself. Listens to close harmony groups, the most irritating music. 'You're devils, both of you, don't think I can't see that. Except you,' he says, pointing to Terry, 'are a less malignant devil than him,' he says, pointing to me. 'They laced my drink, I knew it, I thought I'd pee it out and poison the sewers. What if the internet lost its memory? You'd all be done for.' He flashes a rodent smile, yellow teeth standing out against his white phizog topiary. 'Uh? Uh?' he requests agreement, leaning back on the bed and raising his knees, displaying his nakedness under the gown. 'I don't want a war between heaven and the national health. Life's not fair, God knows it's not fair. It's up to you. Don't think if you're a devil you're worse, you're better. Our Lady gave us an astral present of her immaculate heart and we trashed it.'

We let him out and Greta is there, asking, 'Can I see the guvnor?' I let her todder off, mumbling to herself.

'Did I do good?' Terry asks me.

'It was all right, we did all right.'

'Fearless adventurers, I like the sound of that. We'll find out what's happening. Terry does his homework, that's why he always passes his exams,' he says.

Later in the day, my mother visits. It's hard on her, I know. All this. She talks to me in the recreation room, away from everyone else. She's at the age when she should be relaxing, looking after grandchildren. There's just me and my sister and she's not had any kids yet. My mum used to look young for her age, but after all these problems with the mental health service she looks tired, tired and frail, her brown eyes peering at me with trepidation. She gives me a hug. She's all skin and bone. It hurts me to see her seeing me like this. This is another thing that vampireman has to answer for.

'The tribunal was a fix-up, Mum,' I tell her.

'Have you been taking your medication?' She looks at me sadly. This was a source of arguments when I used to live with her. If you shoved all the scroogies down your screck just like they told you, you'd end up like Rita or Omar. When you've got people on the street who want to kill you, it helps to have voices, keeps you on your toes.

'Course I have, Mum, I'm fine these days. It's you I'm worried about. Why you keep losing weight? Don't worry about fashion, it's health that's number one.' She smiles a little. 'How have you been sleeping, Mum?' I ask. She's been on Mogadon for ages. I used to nick them myself.

'Not so good, Carl, not so good.'

'It's OK here, they feed us, eating our neutrons like good nutjobs.' Her face drops, perhaps an inappropriate choice of words. She's looking at me as if I'm mad. I know it's been hard for her, but that gets me hathed when people do that, start looking at you different, like a switch gets turned on at the back of their brain. I don't let on, though. 'But look at the people here, Mum, half of them can hear Jesus talking to them, you know? There's no way I belong here, it's a travesty.'

I used to steal enough stuff from her. When I was using. Used to skank her and my sister for everything I could take. Say I needed a haircut, trousers for a job interview, money for textbooks. But that was ages ago. My mum's been working as a nurse for a time. I think about how hard she worked for me and my sister and it makes me sorry for her, to see how I turned out.

'When they let me out of here, I'm going to college,' I tell her. 'I reckon a man of my abilities could get a job as a mechanic, at least. And I'm not using no more. Gave that all up myself, no rehab, just stopped. I can sort myself out, no problems.' She listens to me patiently, not wishing to interrupt.

She leaves me some goat curry in an ice-cream box. I share it with Terry, telling him about the visit.

'I've had problems with my mum and all. I'd rather live in a hostel with six hundred cunts, cos at least I know they're cunts, than at home with my mother, who I'm not sure is a cunt,' Terry says. I let that one go. 'Mate, I wanna be a mechanic as well. I've done it before, I know how engines work and everything. We could work together.'

'Yeah, we could do that, Terry.'

'Definitely we'll do that, mate. Terry's had enough of living in a nuthouse.'

★

When I get a decent amount of leave, I head out on a mission. I find myself on the Old Kent Road. You can buy anything there. Rock, brown, charlie, skunk. When I See Things As They Really Are, my life's a lot easier. It's like most people see a train ticket with a green middle and orange strips at the top and bottom. But when I step back, I see the middle's not really green but white with pea-green letters repeatedly saying, *Rail Settlement Plan Rail Settlement Plan Rail Settlement Plan . . .*

But if the unit's your only frame of reference, you get muddled. It's like walking through Red Light Soho, you don't need no pimps swaggering past, menace and charisma, saying 'One love' and 'It's good to be good', when you're confused already, fighting an enemy you can't even see. Outside a café I used to know, I read the sign on the window. It's closed for the night, lit only by the murderous blue gleam of an insectocutor on the wall, my shadow stretching over the empty tables and polished linoleum.

Please do not occupy seats if you are not purchasing food and please do not eat food if it was not purchased from this café.

Up in Epping Forest, that's where I used to go when things got muddled. I could be there days at a time. I'm an outdoors man, see. I would venture deep into the woods at night, until the city lights were a distant shore. In the undergrowth, there's the darkest places, where no one can reach you. I could stand still there for hours, my hunting knife ready, setting traps for rabbits, and it'd be all right. Only noise to bother me would be the railway from miles off. People tell tales about witches there, but I felt safer in Epping than I ever did on the street.

I decide to track down my friend Leon. I met him in a petrol station years back. When I was using. He was in a wheelchair, see, and he only knew a few words. His mum said he had cerebral palsy, because I went back to his house with him. He was about my age. That's what it was, we were friends. I liked him. Didn't have any other friends at the time, real friends anyway. I used to take him out once in a while, and it made his mum really happy that he had someone to talk to. Took him to the park, to the shops. It made me feel good to help him out. It showed me that I wasn't really that ill, relatively speaking.

But when you've got crack cocaine whispering in your ear, it's difficult. That was probably the low point. I took his CD player, flogged it for twenty quid. Twenty fucking quid. Took his benefits book too, but his mum told the police before I could get anything out of it. I had to stand in front of him and his mum in court. My mum too. I don't know how well he understood, but he knew I'd betrayed him.

But I decide to change that. I pass the petrol station and retrace my path down his street. A car goes by, amps booming spectral half-recognizable music, and I stop outside his house, the streetlamp above me having acquired a crimson tint. I want to tell them I'm sorry and how much better I am now. I knock on Leon's door. His mother opens it.

'Hello, Mrs Young. Sorry to disturb you. I'm Carl. You remember me?' I say, smiling as best I can.

Her first look is one of confusion. This is swiftly superseded by surprise and scorn.

'Fucking junkie, get out!'

The door remains ajar just long enough for me to see Leon roll into the hallway. Our eyes meet and I can see how sad and lonely he's been and that he wants to be friends again.

'I'm calling the police,' she screeches through the letter box.

After that, there is just enough time to check my flat before I go back. I reach my block, the skyways blocked because of muggers, puddles on concrete, St George's flags blocking front windows. I walk up to the second floor, avoiding the accusatory glances of my former neighbours. They only know me as the old me.

I get a bad feeling soon as I step in. Something's rotting in the kitchen, a thick sweet odour that clogs your throat. I can hear the pylon outside my window buzzing, as it does incessantly, day and night, day and night. I read somewhere it can give a child leukaemia.

I look in the mirror. I haven't shaved for weeks and the curly black hairs stick together in dirty clumps; the scroogies make my eyes look glazed over, alien. There's rats in the walls too. Or rodents of some species. Whispery clawing through the brickwork, closing in, inch by inch.

'Richard, is it OK to talk to you again?'

Terry is on leave, so I take him to our room alone. Shortly after our last exchange, he cast off his dressing gown and went naked, so they locked him away until he complied. He's dressed in black trousers and a black T-shirt now. It only shows how close the truth was.

'My parents took me to Malta when I was small,' Richard begins. 'Oubliettes, dungeons cut into the rock. They'd push you down through the trapdoor and close you in. My father took me in one, pitch black. They'd throw down scraps and suchlike. Pitch black, darkest place in the world dark, but the prisoners made sculptures. Amazing chariots and horses, ships and houses, all formed from old chicken bones and human excreta melded together. That is awe, Carl. Uh? Uh? Oubliette means forgetter. Remind you of something, does it? Uh? Uh?' he asks, swaying slightly, flashing his yellow incisors.

I let him go then and think about what he said. It must have been the scroogies, because next I'm dreaming. I'm right in front of the rotnut, my nose nearly touching the screen as Anna Ford speaks.

And in Tel Aviv, a suicide bomber blew himself up today, killing twelve bus passengers –

Except she doesn't stop, just plays in a loop. I hear footsteps from the corridor and, when I look up, all the lights are out. The TV is just static, but I can still hear her. The footsteps are getting closer, so I pull back the sofa and crouch between it and the wall. The footsteps reach the door and a nurse is there, the one Terry fancies. Except she's not human. She's got lizard eyes and rows of jagged teeth and a lizard tongue slipping in and out. A vase of flowers on the table withers as she passes, even though I know they're fake because I went up and ran my fingers on the plastic petals.

She goes to turn off the TV, so I slip into the corridor. The pipes are rebelling, metal caterwauling above the ceiling tiles. Light pours out from the gap under a door. It's our room. My hand stretches out for the handle, the pipes pounding above. A movement catches my eye. Greta is silhouetted against the nurses' station, motionless.

'The guvnor,' she whispers, and I hear it over Anna Ford and the pipes.

Our room number is twelve. I wake up. It really is pitch black now. I hear Omar sermonizing in my ear, forcing the words out through his disobedient lips.

'And he for whom Allah has appointed no light, for him there is no light.'

I rise to my feet. Terry Woods. TWelve.

'He's found it out. He's solved it,' they whisper.

Terry's masturbating on his side of the divide, I can hear the rustling. Spreading his toxins into my brain. Filling my muscles with ions and turning them to lead.

'He's going to end it now.'

I slide my bed to block the door and Terry pretends to wake up. I don't turn the lights on yet in case it attracts the draconia.

'Shall I inform you (O people!) upon whom the Shayatin descend? They descend on every lying, sinful person.'

'You think I'm straight off the banana boat,' I shout.

'What?' he murmurs, and I can feel the devil rays coming out of his skull.

'You'll get a taste of your own medicine, you'll see.'

'I'm trying to sleep.'

'Tell me what you've done, Terry, tell me.'

'Sleeping. Deceiving. Fire. Liar.'

I pull the dustbin over and there's a newspaper inside. I set it alight. In the flickering light, I pull out my hunting knife and glimpse his terrified, devious face.

'No, Carl, what's happening?'

'Terry, I'll give you one more chance.'

'Why am I schizophrenia? I'm four years old, watching my dad, who's not really my dad, beating up my mum and my sister with a curtain wire. Why am I schizophrenia? They put me in a care home where the lieutenant is a psychopath, beating the shit out of me, raping me until I left the place. Why am I schizophrenia? I spent half my adult life in prison cells, Carl,' Terry yells.

I turn on the lights. Black smoke clouds the room. I see a tear in Terry's eye. And the scars on his arms.

I freeze, perplexed. I hear the fire alarm's piercing electronic wail.

'He doesn't know the truth. He doesn't know the way.'

After Terry speaks, the door bursts open and two burly male nurses appear. One of them bends my wrist back so I drop the knife and forces me to the floor, while the other stamps out the fire. My face on the carpet, I watch cinders curlicue to the ground.

When they let me out of the psychiatric intensive care unit, I see Greg the old punker, who's come back from busking. He's got black mascara on and a gold mullet with the dye growing out. He wears a skinny-fit Sid Vicious T-shirt that used to be considerably less skinny-fitting before he gained weight in the belly region. The doomed punk scowls on Greg's chest, a bloody criss-cross of self-inflicted wounds adorning his torso. Greg's trying to convince Barry Fishlips that it's his picture on the cover of a 1980 new wave LP.

'The Sex Pistols knew me. They said come along. I used to be among the gang, played with them. I had my own band and that. That's me on the front. I was the singer in my own band. I can give you phone numbers and addresses. Either you believe me or you think I'm mad, it's your choice.'

'I believe you, Greg, I believe you,' I say.

Notes on the Authors

Sylvia Jean Dickinson

I was born in Cape Town, growing up on the Devil's Peak slopes. I then moved to London, married a Yorkshireman and joined him working in Norrtälje, Sweden. In 2003 I was awarded a Creative Writing MA by the University of Chichester. I still live in the area, where I mellow, while my husband golfs. Now sixty, I will travel home alone for six months for research to finish my linked stories/novel.

Crista Ermiya

I was born and grew up in London. My mum is Filipino and my dad is Turkish Cypriot. I now live in Newcastle upon Tyne. People often ask how many languages I can speak, and are disappointed when I say just English. Sometimes I get asked if I can speak English.

Rowena Fan

I was born in England twenty-four years ago, an only child to an irate mother. I grew up and still live in Manchester, where I am surrounded by close and extended family. I have written stories since I was five and have filled many reporters' notebooks since then. I recently had a short story about hair and its cultural significance published in an anthology.

Ahtzaz Hassan

I was born in Pakistan and lived the first eight years of my life near the small town of Jhelum, on the GT Road halfway between Islamabad and Lahore. In 1986 I moved with my parents to London, where I am currently one year away from qualifying as a doctor from the Royal Free and University College London Medical School.

Pauline Kam

Literary age: forty-four. Studied mime in Paris. Worked as a puppeteer using mime, dance and Bunraku techniques. Qualified as a holistic therapist.

I've had a speech disability (laryngeal dystonia) for over thirty years, so I'm delighted to have a 'voice' at last!

Patrice Lawrence

I was born in Brighton, raised in mid-Sussex and live in Hackney, London, with my young daughter. I've written stories since I could write. I have an MA (Distinction) in Writing for Film and TV and have been mentored by the BBC as a prospective comedy writer. I work for a charity and expect never to be rich.

Aoi Matsushima

I was born in Tokyo. Fulfilling the ambition to become a writer in English was the driving force that brought me to the UK in 1997, giving up my ten-year career in PR. After completing an MA in Creative Writing at Bath Spa University College, I won an Ian St James Award (1998) and an Asham Award (1999) for short stories and one of them was published in the Serpent's Tale anthology *Reshape Whilst Damp* (2000). Currently I live in London.

Kachi A. Ozumba

I grew up in Nigeria, where I was born in 1972 (as I was told). My stories have appeared in *BBC Focus on Africa Magazine*, *Gowanus* and *In Posse Review*, where I was the featured writer for the tenth anniversary issue. Currently I live in Wakefield, pursuing an MA in Creative Writing at the University of Leeds while working on my novel, *Cell-Show*.

Saman Shad

I was born in Pakistan but grew up in Australia, as well as spending some time in the Middle East. I'm currently based in London. In addition to writing short stories, I also write plays, which have been produced on BBC Radio London and at the Hampstead Theatre, Theatre 503, Watermans and Kali Theatre, and at the Edinburgh Festival. In 2005 I completed the STARTS writing residency at the Soho Theatre and also had my short story 'Sucking on Tamarind' appear in *Tell Tales Vol. 2*. I'm currently a writer on the BBC radio series *Silver Street* and am working on a novel.

Neil Wellappili

I was born in London and come from a Sri Lankan background. Currently I am studying alongside Mr Ahtzaz Hassan. In Kingston, I live with my family. I have written other stories and scripts, and aim to learn from my mistakes.